My name is Callum Ormond.
I am undercover on Shadow Island.
My story continues...

BLACK OPS

CONSPIRACY 365

HUNTED

To Alex

First American Edition 2013
Kane Miller, A Division of EDC Publishing

Text copyright © Gabrielle Lord, 2013
Cover design copyright © Scholastic Australia, 2013
Cover design and internal graphics by Nicole Stofberg
Cover logo designed by Natalie Winter

First published by Scholastic Australia Pty Limited in 2013
This edition published under license from Scholastic Australia Pty Limited.

Cover photography: Cal by Wendell Levi Teodoro (www.zeduce.org) © Scholastic
Australia 2013; volcano © photos.com/Ammit; volcanic eruption © shutterstock.com/
Vulkanette; orange explosion © istockphoto.com/Lisa Anderson; gray smoke and ash
cloud © istockphoto.com/Warren Goldswain; fire © shutterstock.com /mironov; fire
© shutterstock.com /a-poselenov; river and trees © shutterstock.com/Steffen Foerster;
extra trees © shutterstock.com/Nickolay Stanev.
Internal photography and illustration: crate on page 175 © istockphoto.com/
stocksnapper; world map on pages 170–169 © istockphoto.com/pop_jop; string on
world map on pages 170–169 © shutterstock.com/Picsfive; folder and documents on
page 165 © istockphoto.com/subjug; map on pages 142–141 © istockphoto.com/Eric
Scafetta; icons on pages 142–141 © photos.com/John Takai/art12321/Lumumba/joingate;
phone on pages 062 and 051 ©fotolia.com/L_amica.

For information contact:
Kane Miller, A Division of EDC Publishing
PO Box 470663
Tulsa, OK 74147-0663
www.kanemiller.com
www.edcpub.com
www.usbornebooksandmore.com

Library of Congress Control Number: 2013939411

Printed and bound in the United States of America
1 2 3 4 5 6 7 8 9 10
ISBN: 978-1-61067-171-2

HUNTED

GABRIELLE LORD

Kane Miller
A DIVISION OF EDC PUBLISHING

PREVIOUSLY...

DAY 1

Ryan has disappeared, leaving a note saying he's with new friends. I receive a strange text message showing a world map with a skull and crossbones and the words "90 days" written on it. That night, I'm attacked on the street and knocked unconscious.

DAY 2

I'm subjected to a series of terrifying tests and discover that a secret government organization, SI-6, wants to recruit me to go on an undercover mission. I'll be sent to a youth retreat on Shadow Island to check on a missing girl. I agree because they believe Ryan is also on the island.

DAY 8

SI-6 briefs me on the natural dangers on the island and their suspicions that all may not be what it seems at the resort there.

DAY 16

After a few days of paraglider training at SI-6 and being delayed due to bad weather, I finally leave for Shadow Island. I make a terrifying night-landing there.

DAY 17

I find Ryan and discover he has serious concerns about the island's new leader, Damien Thoroughgood. I swap places with him and make contact with Sophie, the missing girl, who decides to help me in my mission to find out the truth about Shadow Island.

DAY 23

I try to blend in as "Ryan" at the Paradise People Resort and work hard to impress Damien. As more and more things seem suspicious, my concerns continue to grow.

DAY 28

I'm training in the elite athletic squad, The Edge. I notice people are going missing and Sophie has also disappeared. I come across kids in the jungle and follow them into a secret bunker underneath a mountain and watch them training. I find a network of tunnels and caves, and steal a motorboat to visit the rocky outcrop where a prisoner is rumored to be held. The rumor is true, but the prisoner doesn't remember who he is and someone arrives before I can try to free him. Back on shore, I receive a mysterious message about Sophie.

DAY 29

Ryan and I meet Zak and Ariel, runaways who have been living in the jungle. We work together to figure out what Damien is up to and where the missing kids might be. We try to rescue Sophie, but our plan fails.

DAY 30

I sneak into Damien's office, steal a key and finally free Sophie. Back in the jungle, we're spied on by a robot python. Ryan manages to obtain a master key so I can get back into Damien's office to download secret information from his computer. But I see Damien returning before I'm finished, dragging Ryan with him. I'm trapped with no way to avoid coming face-to-face with Ryan and revealing my presence on the island to Damien.

DAY 30

61 days to go . . .

Damien Thoroughgood's Office

8:16 pm

I hurled myself away from the desk as footsteps clanged on the metal stairs outside. In my panic, I knocked over a statue next to the keyboard, and just when I thought things couldn't get any worse, they did. The statue must have hit a hot key, activating an alarm. Flashing red lights and a deafening siren screamed through the building. A running banner of green lights on the wall opposite the desk flashed a message:

ESCAPE HATCH ACTIVATED

Escape hatch? *Where?* Frantically, I looked around the room.

It was so discreet, I almost missed it. A small square hatch had popped open, low down in the wall behind the desk. Outside the office, the noises on the staircase grew louder as Ryan was hauled up to Damien's office—right where I stood, frantic to escape before our double act was uncovered!

The hatch was already closing.

This was my only chance.

I dived through as the hatch closed, the door catching one of my feet. With a swift tug, I freed myself and the hatch clicked tight behind me.

I was in a tiny crawl space. Maybe I could hide in this little hole until it was safe to come out again. Beyond the wall, footsteps thudded past me into the office. I could barely hear their voices over the screaming siren.

"Shut that noise off!" I heard someone yell, and almost immediately the siren stopped. Now I could hear the conversation in the adjoining room clearly.

"What's going on?" bellowed Damien.

"Someone set off the alarm," a voice said.

"You!" Damien yelled, obviously at my brother. "Sit there and don't move. I'll deal with you in a moment." I imagined Ryan sitting as he was ordered, probably wondering where I was, with no idea that I was hiding on the other side of the wall, less than three feet away from him.

"It's a false alarm," said Damien after a pause. "This statue fell over on my desk. It must have triggered it."

I breathed a sigh of relief. The green lights of the escape hatch signal must have also turned off. I hoped that no one would think of checking behind the escape hatch, where I crouched, listening through the wall.

"Ryan, I want some answers from you. What were you doing up there in the rainforest?" Damien asked.

"I saw a snake," said Ryan. "It was hanging around near the beach, where we pull up the kayaks. I was chasing it away farther up into the jungle and I kind of got lost."

"Is that the truth? Or were you helping the runaways?" Damien said suspiciously.

"No, sir. I don't know what you mean. I was just worried about the snake scaring some of the younger kids," said Ryan quietly.

"Ryan, I'm very disappointed in you. I really thought you had the makings of an outstanding elite athlete and a member of the top team. But I'm having second thoughts about your attitude.

Take him to your office, Hamish. I'll leave it up to you to decide whether or not Ryan deserves to be at the next level."

"Please," begged Ryan. "Ever since I joined The Edge, it's been my dream to get to the top level, so I can try out the awesome rock climbing and jungle adventuring I keep hearing such amazing things about."

I heard the sound of chairs being pushed back and footsteps moving away. Their voices faded as the door slammed shut behind them, while Ryan continued to protest his innocence down the corridor.

The office was now empty. I hoped Ryan would be all right. If Ryan made the Zenith team—the final level of training, where kids were admitted to the exclusive and secret arena inside the mountain—then maybe I could learn more about what was going on. But I didn't want him to do that if it meant risking his own safety.

I promised myself that I'd come back to check on Ryan as soon as I could. But first I had to get out of the mess I was in right now. How was I going to get out of the office and escape undetected? I couldn't risk "Ryan" reappearing in Damien's office. Not now.

In the uncomfortably cramped space, I noticed three dim lights on the wall near my elbow. I looked closer. Each light had a label on it and it dawned on me then that the escape hatch wasn't just a hole in the wall—it was an elevator! I studied the labels for a moment—1 and 2 were easy enough to understand—they were the first floor below and the second floor at Damien's office. *So B must be for basement?* If I didn't want to run the risk of using the main stairs, I'd have to give it a shot. I pressed B.

There was a slight jolt and then I was descending with a soft hum. Within a few moments, the elevator stopped and one of its sides slid open. I peered out. I was in a dim, underground space, partly filled with what looked like cartons of supplies. Cautiously, I climbed out and straightened up, rubbing my back and taking in my surroundings. I poked around in a few boxes, wondering if there might be food, but it was all paper and equipment.

There was a dark corridor leading off into impenetrable blackness. It reminded me of being inside the mountain, behind the secret entrance in the jungle. All was still and silent. I looked around for CCTV cameras, but there weren't any. With the light from my phone, I started to make my way down the dark corridor. Was I walking into a trap? Was someone expecting me after the alarm had tripped? I didn't have much choice. I kept following the tunnel between the thick rock walls.

Unknown Tunnel System

8:44 pm

As I walked in farther, a deep rumble from the depths of the earth growled through the tunnel, and a second later, the ground shivered underneath my feet. Then the jolting stopped as suddenly as it had started. I waited a moment, but nothing more came. I kept going, deeper and deeper into the darkness.

It didn't take me long to start wondering if this underground hide-out was connected to the mountain lair where I'd seen the Zenith team training and the secret harbor that led out to the ocean. It seemed as if the whole of Shadow Island was riddled with tunnels—some natural, others obviously man-made, hewn from the rock.

I discovered some of these tunnels were short and led only to dead ends. I found one huge storeroom filled with military-looking equipment in crates and under tarpaulins. On the side of one crate was some lettering. I wasn't sure what it meant, so I took a photo and made a mental note to send it to Boges when I was back above ground.

The tunnel I was walking through had a derelict, unused look to it—which suited me just fine. I had no desire to meet anyone else. Just as I approached the entrance to a larger tunnel, the light of my phone suddenly failed. I was plunged into midnight blackness. Fumbling in the dark, I pressed all the buttons I could find, but it was dead. *Great.*

I leaned against a hard wall and tried to think. I was completely lost in a labyrinth of crisscrossing tunnels, and I couldn't see a thing. I'd have to feel my way through. But through to *where?*

Slowly, I started feeling along the rough surface, hoping to find the entrance to the wider tunnel I'd spotted just before the light went out. Shuffling along, my hands patting forward along the walls, I found myself patting air. This must be it! I followed the curved sides along for a while then came to another corner. I turned with it and kept going.

9:32 pm

It was hot and humid in the tunnels, and I pulled off my hoodie, tying the sleeves around my waist. I stumbled along in the pitch darkness, feeling my way like some kind of underground caterpillar. I thought I could hear a faint humming sound in the distance and aimed for it. I hoped it would give me some clues as to where I was in the underground maze.

Soon, the humming seemed closer. I moved towards it. My foot struck something and I was jerked forward, banging my head against something solid. I started running my hands over it. *It's a vehicle of some sort*, I thought, as I patted around in the dark, my hands moving over huge, fat wheels. They were attached to some steps and a platform, with some kind of roll bar running all around and what felt like an open cabin.

I climbed onto the platform above the wheels and groped around, trying to interpret the strange vehicle through my hands. It was very big. There was a dashboard at what I presumed was the front of the machine. I ran my fingers over it, trying to get a sense of what kind of vehicle I'd blundered into. As I did so, I must have knocked a switch because a blinding light came on and I was jolted forward.

What was happening? Another earthquake?

This wasn't an earthquake. In a flash I realized I had somehow activated this heavy mining machine. It reminded me a little of the Mars rover, only ten times bigger! There was a blazing light shining down from the top of its cabin, a massive drum-like circular cutting blade at the front and a monitor mounted on the dashboard. I peered at the screen. It showed the wall the machine was heading straight for!

Pixels on the screen twinkled, as if sections of the rock face were moving. *How can a rock face move?* But I had no more time to wonder about that. If I couldn't stop the vehicle, it would crash straight into the wall.

I frantically pushed buttons on the console, but the rover rumbled angrily and insistently towards the solid rock face. I gave up any chance of controlling it and was about to jump off when the rover suddenly stopped—only inches from the rock face. *I must have gotten lucky with one of the buttons*, I thought with relief.

I climbed down, and by the light shining from the front of the vehicle, I investigated my surroundings. To the side of the rover, a steel door with a small window at head height caught my attention. What lay behind it seemed to be the source of the humming I'd heard earlier. As I approached it, the small window lit up. My movements had triggered an automatic light inside. It revealed a very well-equipped laboratory, where automated scientific equipment moved through their processing cycles.

Other movement caught my eye and I saw a number of transparent sea creatures pulsing away in a row of fluid-filled containers stretching along the side lab bench. I wondered if they were Irukandji jellyfish, captured by Damien in order to study them. What was going on in this underground lab? Shadow Island was harboring more secrets than I could have imagined.

As I stepped back, the lights went out inside the laboratory. At my approach, the lights flashed on again and I tried the door handle, but it was locked. I took another look inside. There were lab benches and sinks, Bunsen burners, several fume cupboards and a scattering of scientific glass bottles and test tubes lying around. Someone had been here recently. I jumped when I realized I still had the master key, safely zipped up in my hoodie pocket. I pulled it out and tried it in the lock.

Secret Laboratory

9:40 pm

Slowly, the door opened and I stepped inside. I went over to the sea creatures. They didn't look like Irukandji. I'd never seen anything like these before—they were about an inch wide, shaped like miniature stingrays, gently moving through the water. I turned to the long, central-island lab bench, where dozens of small cubes with rounded corners made an untidy heap almost along its whole length. They looked like kids' building blocks. Did scientists play with blocks? But then I saw that these were no ordinary blocks. Tiny lights winked on some of them while others had small symmetrical openings in them, like the narrow slits of a power outlet.

I hated my phone for giving up right at the worst time. I felt sure Boges would know what these blocks were for, but I couldn't send him a photo. Pinned on a board above one of the long benches running around the laboratory was a map of the world.

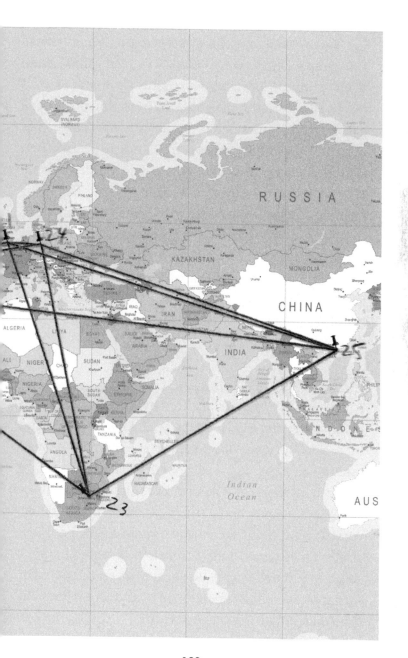

There were lengths of string stretched across the map. There were also five red pins, each with a small handwritten symbol next to it. I frowned, trying to make sense of it. The pins were stuck into well-known major cities—there was one in New York, others in London, Frankfurt, Johannesburg and the last one in Hong Kong. Maybe they were airline routes, I thought.

I stretched up to see what was written next to the nearest pin. It was Johannesburg and I could just make out a letter and a number: *Z3*. I couldn't see the others unless I climbed up on the lab bench and I didn't want to risk doing that. Z3—Johannesburg. I wondered what that might mean.

9:50 pm

I turned my attention to the five very large backpacks, more like military rucksacks, standing in a row on the floor under the map. I peered inside the first one and poked around cautiously at its contents. At the top, I could see a pair of coveralls, some tools in a wraparound holder, what looked like food rations and a small package of sterile gloves. Daring to reach farther inside, I could see there was a large, sealed envelope with serrated security tape across it and the words *Do Not Open Until Command*. Huh?

I kept searching and saw ropes, protein packs and tablets. "Decontamination," I read aloud. "Allow to dissolve in water before drinking." In a side pocket, I spotted the edge of a passport. I pulled it out and opened it—Georgia Montgomery; DOB 10.14.96.

If this was Georgia Montgomery's rucksack, where was Georgia Montgomery? Was she one of the missing people?

Quickly, I checked the other four rucksacks. They were identical—filled with rations, tools, water decontamination tablets, coveralls, and each with a sealed envelope and passport. I reached in to have a look at another passport, but something made me freeze. I thought I heard voices coming along the tunnel. I strained to hear. Was it just my imagination working overtime? I was spooked now.

Hastily, I stole to the doorway and listened hard, all the while looking at the rucksacks. Where were their owners? What was in the sealed envelopes? Perhaps the Zenith team were going to do some survival field practice? But they wouldn't need passports for that. Shadow Island offered all sorts of challenges to survival already.

When I was convinced that no one was coming, I turned my attention back to the lab, and started pulling open a few cupboards. I found more lab equipment, but inside one cupboard, another smaller glass-fronted cupboard had been installed. The key dangled temptingly in its lock. Cautiously, I turned the key and opened it. Inside was a small metal box. I lifted out the box and eased open the lid. On the underside, the words *Biosurge—caution—use only under medical supervision* were written in bold red letters.

I lifted out a small package of pills in blister packs, except these were no ordinary pills. Instead each blister held a small oval pellet, not much bigger than a grain of rice. Up close, I could see that they were covered in tiny holes. I pulled out my Swiss Army knife and very carefully cut one off. Hopefully it would never be noticed. What was Biosurge?

Curious, I put the box back in its cupboard and was about to lock it when I spotted a slim folder, almost invisible as it lay flat on the higher shelf.

Looking around, and pausing to hear if anyone was coming, I reached up and grabbed it, flicking it open. It contained a couple of pages of computer printout, but I was deeply disappointed. It didn't seem to be the amazing information I was hoping would explain all these strange things. It might be important, but I couldn't understand what it meant.

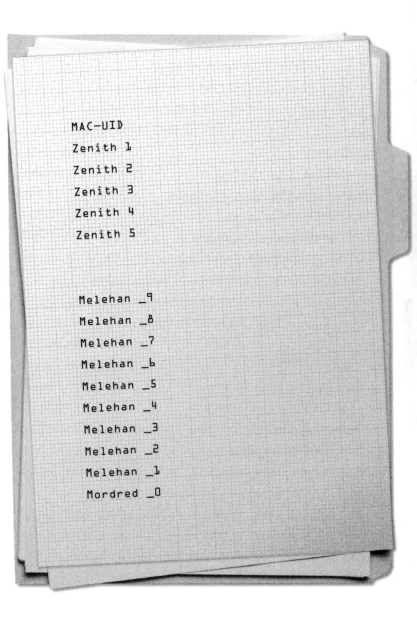

MAC-UID
Zenith 1
Zenith 2
Zenith 3
Zenith 4
Zenith 5

Melehan _9
Melehan _8
Melehan _7
Melehan _6
Melehan _5
Melehan _4
Melehan _3
Melehan _2
Melehan _1
Mordred _0

Mordred! That name again.

I hated my phone even more for dying on me. I memorized the codes to send to Boges later.

Reluctantly, I put the folder back on the top shelf and locked the cupboard, leaving the keys dangling as they were before, closing the outer cupboard.

When I opened the next cupboard, I reeled back in horror! Five human eyes were glaring at me! *What the...*

I blinked. They were still staring at me, shining out from light boxes, like those used by doctors to check X-rays. Then I looked again. I realized with relief that they weren't real eyes, but incredibly deceptive holograms. Each one was a different color—hazel, brown, blue, green and gray. Were they some kind of robotic eye? But why only one of each? I tried to get my head around it, but couldn't.

I stood in the middle of the lab, looking around me. Five rucksacks, five red pins, five holographic eyes. Five people going to five different cities with these strange supplies. I felt confused and now, something else as well. I realized I could feel a knot churning in my gut. Fear. Something I couldn't understand was happening, and I knew it was wrong. And it was right before my very own eyes.

10:01 pm

Maybe the glossy brochures I'd noticed earlier lying on a counter might contain some useful information. I took the top one off the pile and turned to the first page.

"Thoroughgood Advanced Robotics," I read. "Search and Rescue (SAR) Applications for Multiple Terrains." Maybe the 3-D eyes were some kind of new robotic camera eye design, to be used in SAR work? I remembered Dad saying that the human eye and a camera's "eye" simply don't see the same things. Was Thoroughgood Robotics working on improving that?

I flipped through to the end of the brochure, but there was nothing about Biosurge. I'll try to make sense of it later, I thought, as I shoved it in my pocket. A slight movement near the ceiling in the center of the lab caught my attention. I looked up, and saw something that made me flinch and jump back. I raced out the door.

The lights went out. They came on again as I ventured closer to take another look. There, dangling from one of the light fixtures in the ceiling, looking straight at me through the window in the door with its beady eyes, was another robot snake. I ducked to the left, and it was frightening the way its head snaked around to follow my actions. Right this very minute it might be beaming images of me deep inside the tunnel-infested mountain onto a monitor somewhere. I was willing to bet that the screens in Damien's office that I'd thought showed hand-held cameras were feeds from two of these surveillance pythons—*spythons*, more like—as they slithered around spying and sending back live footage from their tiny, beady-eyed cameras!

That thought spurred me into action. I needed to leave, right now. But before I could move, I heard voices in the distance. I was sure this time, as the sound echoed eerily through the dark tunnels. Desperately, I looked around for somewhere to hide. There was only one place—I'd have to squeeze myself between the squat rover vehicle and the side of the tunnel. I scrambled into position, avoiding the huge cutting blades on the front of the machine, hoping that the housing on the vehicle's motor would provide sufficient cover.

The voices came closer. I could even identify them. It was Damien and his second-in-command, Hamish. I could smell food. Were they going to have a late-night feast in the tunnels?

Moments later, I heard them coming to the area near the laboratory and then I saw the flickering light of a flashlight.

"The machine's moved!" Damien called out.

A flashlight beam swerved closer to me and I squeezed back even farther, gritting my teeth as the huge cutting blades of the rover pressed up against my skin. The light lingered on the stony ground near me and then moved up and away across the walls. Abruptly, the beam of light swung around in the opposite direction.

"No one's been down here," said Hamish. Then after a pause he added, "I guess it could have been activated by an earthquake. It has a very sensitive ignition switch." Damien grunted.

Thank you, Hamish.

Spying from my hiding place, I saw the two of them go to the door of the lab. The automatic lights came on inside. I heard Damien say, "Everything looks in order. But the modbots have moved."

"Jeffrey would be pleased to know that," said Hamish as they moved away.

Modbots? What were they talking about? Jeffrey was Damien's brother, the man who had set up the Paradise People Resort. Why would *he* be pleased?

10:19 pm

A few seconds later, they had vanished down the main tunnel, but not before I'd spotted the food containers Hamish and Damien were carrying.

Cautiously, I crept out, intending to follow them. It was the only way I could get out of there, even though I was risking them doubling back and running straight into me. I had to make sure that didn't happen.

Keeping well back, I followed the small glow of their flashlight through the maze of black tunnels.

Gradually, the aroma of food wafting back to me mixed with the smell of the sea. The atmosphere in the tunnel had changed—the air was fresher, saltier and less oppressive. Grayish light filled the tunnel ahead of me, but Damien and Hamish had disappeared from sight. I suddenly realized what they were doing. They must be taking food to someone! But why such a large amount of food?

Of course! Ryan and Sophie had told me about the kids who just vanished. They must be imprisoned deep inside the mountain after all! I hurried to catch up with Hamish and Damien, following the dim light and their distant voices.

Once, I came around a corner too quickly and almost crashed into them—they must have stopped to discuss something. Quickly, I jumped back.

"What was that?" Damien asked.

I flattened myself against the wall, trying to

melt into the hard surface.

"Probably just rats," said Hamish.

I heard Damien take a step in my direction. *Don't come any closer.*

I was too scared to breathe, fearing that he would sense the movement of air even if he didn't see me. There was a long pause.

"Maybe we do have rats," said Damien. I cringed back, desperately trying to be invisible. The beam of light came closer, playing all over the wall and on the ground nearby. "The generator should be fixed by now, Hamish. How much longer is it going to take to get the lighting system in this section of the tunnel working again? I don't care for all this stumbling around in the dark."

"I'm waiting on a part from the mainland; there was a delay in ordering it. It should be on the supply ship next week, sir."

"Make sure it's given top priority. Another sixty days, Hamish," Damien said, "and we won't have to be running this room service anymore. The first five are ready to go and the others need just a little more polishing of their skills." He laughed and it was an ugly sound.

"They'll need them where they're going!" Hamish grunted.

The first five? And what others? Pushing all

my questions to the back of my mind, I focused on shadowing them down the tunnel. I heard the jangling of keys and dared to creep a little closer. Sure enough, Damien was opening a door farther along the tunnel. He and Hamish disappeared inside. What was Damien planning to do with the prisoners after sixty days? This *had* to be related to the countdown on his computer. And the text message I'd received. I had to find out.

I could smell the sea clearly now and even hear its dim roar echoing down the tunnel. Common sense told me I needed to make a run for it while they were in the room. Crouching low, I sneaked along the tunnel towards the door. A dim light shone through the small glass window as I ducked past. Once on the other side, I couldn't resist waiting next to the wall, hoping to eavesdrop on their conversation. I was in luck.

". . . and make sure you pull that Ryan kid into line," Damien said. I could hear him opening a cupboard door.

"I'm letting him cool his heels tonight and I'll sort him out in the morning," Hamish replied. "Don't worry about him, that one's just a bit headstrong, but we'll soon have him under control." I silently thanked the universe that Ryan had not been hurt. At least Hamish didn't seem as ruthless as Damien. But my thanks were short-lived.

"We'll see. But I want a line search at first light. I want every bit of this island combed until we find them. Especially Sophie Bellamy. She must not be allowed to get away. She and the others must be captured. Then they can join the happy throng down here. I'll be explaining at roll call that the runaways have a serious infection and it's essential to track them down and find them before the illness gets too bad," Damien said.

An infection? I crept closer, listening with disbelief.

"Those good-hearted idiots—our little 'Paradise People'—won't rest until they've tracked them down to 'save' them."

"How long will the search go on for, sir?"

"As long as it takes, Hamish. They must be found."

"But that could take days, weeks maybe."

"Whatever it takes. Got it? And pass me some of those water bottles, will you?"

Now I understood what Damien was up to. He was going to tell a complete lie to the people back at the resort so that they'd leave no stone unturned until they found us to save us from a non-existent sickness. And the really horrible thing about the lie was that the Paradise People would think they were *helping* the runaways.

And Damien wasn't going to give up until he'd found us. Day after day we'd be in danger of being discovered. It would be OK to avoid them for a while, but what if it went on for weeks?

My thoughts were interrupted by Hamish's voice. "But won't the kids at the resort worry that they might catch it?"

"I'll hand out some sugar pills tomorrow—tell them it's a powerful antibiotic that will protect them completely from the infection. That should allay any worries."

I had to jump back as they came towards the door. Time to go! The smell of the sea told me I was somewhere close to a way out. I kept flat against the rock face as I followed the salty scent. Soon the roar of the sea lashing the coast got louder. When I finally emerged, I realized I was at the submersible wharf. All these tunnels must be interconnected!

I made a mental note of the position of the tunnel from which I'd just come. That was the one we'd need to search to discover where the prisoners were being held. But I needed to get back to Zak, Ariel and Sophie and tell them about what I'd seen in the tunnels and in Damien's office. I wanted to get their thoughts on what I'd discovered in the lab—the rucksacks, the mysterious Biosurge pellets, the staring holographic eyes . . .

Across the cavern, opposite to where I was crouching, the streamlined submersible bobbed gently on the swell, gleaming in the evening light.

Shadow Island Jungle

11:12 pm

After the long, arduous climb over the rocks from the cavern entrance, it was hot and sticky as I made my way through the undergrowth and the jungle.

Instinctively, I ended up at the familiar old convicts' cemetery. All of a sudden, fatigue overwhelmed me. This had been one of the longest days—and nights—of my life. I couldn't imagine dragging my tired body any farther. And besides, surely I'd be safe for tonight. There was hardly going to be a search party coming for me now. I'd call BB tomorrow once I'd had time to put all the crazy things I'd seen into some kind of order in my mind.

I found a hidden spot under a large tree and lay down between the sprawling roots. Even if I just lay here for an hour or two, I thought, then I can make my way back to the Katz cave. I closed my eyes and sank into a dreamless sleep.

DAY 31
60 days to go . . .

Next thing I knew, the birds were calling overhead and the sun was making itself felt. I sat up in a momentary daze. The events of the day before washed over me like a crashing surf . . . rescuing Sophie, hiding in the jungle, sneaking into Damien's office, stumbling through the dark maze of tunnels and the secrets I'd found there.

I stretched my stiff legs, then started heading for the resort compound. I needed to find out what was happening with Ryan and Hamish. As I came closer, I could hear people already playing volleyball on the beach. I could also see the dark pennant flying on the flagpole. The Edge training was on.

My mind boggled at how carefree most of the kids were, completely unaware of what lay underneath their feet in the tunnels below. Carefully, I made my way towards the fence, looking for a hidden spot to climb over.

Paradise People Resort

7:19 am

I knew that Hamish's office was a small room next to the stores building, away from the beach side of the resort. Staying down, I made my way through the last of the undergrowth until I could see part of the wall and the half-opened window of his office. Looking each way, I crept to the window, flattening myself against the wall. I figured there was no reason for anyone to come around the back and that I was unlikely to be seen if I was careful.

I could hear Hamish's voice. ". . . and Damien needs to know that you are completely committed to being a team member, Ryan. You know what that means."

"Hard training and no more wandering off after snakes in the jungle, I've got it," said Ryan. I could tell he was putting on a good show of remorse for Hamish.

"More than that. It's time that your group met the final challenge."

"Do you mean CQC?" Ryan's voice again. *What were they talking about?*

"Even more than CQC," said Hamish. "After the final training session, committed members will get their vitamin implants and their elite tattoos to become full members of the Zenith team. You'll be like an Olympian on Shadow Island. That's something to really strive for."

"I really want that, Hamish," said Ryan. "To be the best that I can be. *Please*."

"I'm not completely sure about you, Ryan. You seem to have a bit of a split personality," said Hamish slowly. "But I'm prepared to give you another chance."

Split personality? I hoped he wasn't getting suspicious.

"I need to know that you are fully committed."

"One thousand percent."

"No more irregular behavior?"

"No way. I'll be as regular as can be."

"Good. Wait here while I go get my gear and then we'll rejoin the others."

I heard him leave the office and as soon as I was sure he was out of earshot, I tapped on the glass. Ryan jumped to his feet and came to the window.

"Cal! What are you doing here?"

"Checking up on you. What happened?"

"I got caught not far from the cemetery last night and Damien dragged me back to his office. I tried telling him I was just lost in the jungle, but he wasn't buying it this time."

"He thought you were taking food to the

runaways," I grinned, finding some relief from the fear and tension of the tunnels in joking with my brother, "and you answered in your really polite school voice that you didn't know what he was talking about."

Ryan's eyes widened. "How do you know that?"

"I'm psychic," I said, making the most of his bewilderment.

"OK, mind reader, what happened next?" Ryan demanded.

I sneaked to the end of the building and peered around the corner. There was no one coming and a loud cheer from the direction of the beach told me that everyone was down there, enjoying themselves. I came back to the window.

"Damien told you to go with Hamish who would talk to you about your attitude in his office," I said.

I could see Ryan's disbelief as I repeated almost word for word what had happened in Damien's office. Then I burst out laughing. It broke the rest of the tension that I'd been feeling. "Sorry, bro," I finally confessed, "I'm not psychic. I went through a little escape hatch and was hiding in the wall near Damien's desk."

"You were in Thoroughgood's office?" Ryan asked in disbelief.

I nodded.

"An escape hatch? In the wall?" Ryan asked, amazed.

"I haven't got time to explain everything now. I just wanted to make sure you were OK. What's been happening? I only overheard the last part."

"Hamish tore into me, telling me how I was wasting a fantastic once-in-a-lifetime chance, that I had a great talent and that I was throwing it away. So I looked real sad and sorry and asked for one last chance—again. I convinced him that I was totally committed to becoming a top-ranking Zenith team member."

"You've got to be really careful, Ryan. Hamish will be watching you like a hawk." Instantly, I knew I'd said the wrong thing.

"I can take care of myself. You're not the only one who's done it tough, you know," Ryan said huffily.

"I know that," I said quickly. "What's CQC?" I asked, changing the subject.

"I heard one of the other elite squad kids talking about it—it means 'close quarters combat.' That's the last level of training for the Zenith team," Ryan said.

"And then you get some kind of implant? Do you know what Hamish was talking about?" I asked.

"Yeah, he'd been lecturing me about the importance of it earlier. The implant is supposed to take the place of months of training. He said it would improve my performance out of sight. It's supposed to deliver measured doses of a new, completely safe, performance-enhancing mix of vitamins and other natural ingredients. At least, that's what he told me. But if it's just a dose of vitamins and natural supplements, why all the bother with implants?"

"I don't like the sound of this at all," I said. "The implant must be what makes those wounds we've seen on the Zenith kids."

"I can handle myself, Cal," Ryan said.

"I know you can. But what are you going to do when it comes time to get the implant?" I replied.

"I'll think of something," said Ryan. "Stop stressing." He paused and looked straight into my eyes. "You don't think I can do it, do you?" he said. "You don't think I'll make it to the top Zenith level."

"Hey, that's not true. Of course you can do it. You're fully fit now that your ankle's healed. And it was awesome how you got that master key from Elmore. I know you're strong and smart."

"That's right. Just because you're a few minutes older than I am doesn't mean I need a big brother around all the time, looking over my shoulder, taking care of me."

"Hey, Ryan," I said. "It's not like that. I'm really stoked that you and I found each other through the whole Ormond Singularity thing. I know you did some amazing things to help me when you barely knew me, leading the authorities away from me when I was totally exhausted and couldn't run anymore. It's only natural . . ." I stopped. I could see he wasn't listening to me anymore.

"I'm going to start close quarters combat training. I'll think of a way to get out of the implant," Ryan repeated.

I was going to say more, but sometimes it was best just to let things go. "Can I borrow your phone?" I asked Ryan.

He handed it over and said, "See? You need me, Cal."

"Of course I need you," I said. "You're my brother," I said.

I called Boges, but it went straight to voice mail. I left a message, hoping that Boges would get back to me soon with some brilliant ideas about the information I'd hacked and sent to him and BB. Whatever it was, we needed to know what the Mordred key file contained. And I wanted to tell him about the strange list of Zenith numbers and names I'd found in the folder locked away in the secret laboratory.

As I handed the phone back to Ryan, I heard someone coming around the back of the building! I dived into the undergrowth and hid, peering out from some thick, leafy cover. It was Hamish. I watched him walk to the window through which I had just been talking to Ryan. He stood there, looking around. Had he heard our voices? I saw him look down and I groaned under my breath. My sneakers had left impressions in the soft rainforest soil beneath the window. Hamish frowned, looked around and then vanished back around the corner.

Shadow Island Jungle

7:37 am

I kept thinking about my brother as I climbed back up through the rainforest to Zak and Ariel's cave. Sometimes Ryan drove me crazy— like the way he'd just dropped out and joined the Paradise People. I worried that if he refused the implant, he might end up like the other reluctant kids, locked up somewhere. I sure didn't want that to happen.

I thought of Hamish, checking out the footprints in the mud beneath the window of his office. There was no way he could know whose footprints they were. All he could know was that someone—any one of the kids at the resort—had been outside the window.

After a hot and steamy climb, I found the familiar jungle clearing and the clump of tangled undergrowth that told me I was in the right place. Moments later, I was lifting the thick overhang away.

Katz Cave

8:05 am

Three scared, shocked faces swung my way as I crawled into the wide, dry cave. Zak jumped up at my stealthy entrance. "Cal! Where have you been? We were so worried!"

"What happened?" Sophie asked as Ariel gave me a bear hug.

I told them how I'd nearly been caught in Damien's office as he hauled Ryan in to explain why he was out in the jungle.

"So where's Ryan?" Sophie asked. "Is he OK?" Her concern for my brother was obvious in her face.

I hesitated a moment before answering. "He's OK," I said. "I managed to sneak a visit to him just then. He's convinced Hamish to give him a second chance. A third chance, really. He's aiming to make the final Zenith team level."

"But the initiation!" cried Sophie. "He's not going to do that, is he?"

"Hamish told him it's just an implant. But Ryan says he'll think of a way to get out of it," I said.

"But how? We all got in real trouble when we refused to have it," Sophie said.

Zak and Ariel nodded in agreement.

I had no answer to that, so instead I told them about stealing into Damien's office thanks to the master key. I noticed the look of admiration on Sophie's face as I explained to the others how Ryan had lifted the key from Elmore's collection and put it under his mattress for me to find.

"That was cool," Sophie smiled and Ariel grinned, nudging her.

As I hungrily ate some fruit, I explained about discovering the Mordred key file on Damien's laptop, and using the Stealth Hacker to get the file and send it off to SI-6 and Boges. I told them about the painfully slow download and how I'd nearly gone nuts with nerves, especially when I'd seen Ryan being brought in by Damien and his cronies.

"I knew once they saw the two of us together," I said, "it'd be the end of our double act." I told them about accidentally activating the emergency system, and how I just managed to get through the secret hatch with literally seconds to spare as Damien burst into the room with Ryan. I described my journey all the way down to the basement level and my discovery of the tunnels that crisscrossed under the mountain. I described all the stores I'd found and the "Live Ordnance" crate.

"That means live ammunition," said Zak.

"Oh no," I said. "What would they want that for?" This was getting much worse.

8:20 am

I told them about crashing into the rover vehicle which somehow activated it. They were fascinated by what I'd seen in the laboratory—the strange blinking blocks, the sea creatures in the glass containers, the map with its marked routes, the rucksacks filled with rations and a passport, the piece of paper pinned to Johannesburg—Z3.

"Now I'm thinking it could be something to do with the Zenith team," I suggested as I came to the end of my description of the lab. "Hey, Ariel?" I said. "Do you still have your map of the island?"

She nodded and fished the crumpled paper out of a nearby crate.

"I'll mark up some of those extra tunnels while I can remember them," I said.

rock
secret entrance
CG
RESORT
Damien's office
tunnels
mooring cave in
who is here?

WELCOME TO
the real SHADOW
ISLAND

volcano

W-W

We sat in silence for a while, each of us trying to understand what was going on. "I should also mention," I said, "that there's a light box in one of the cupboards and it contains five eyes."

"*What?!*" they all chorused at once.

"They were holograms," I said. "I got a real shock, too, when I saw them."

"Could it be something to do with robotics?" Zak asked. "Special eye cameras or something like that?"

I shrugged. "I wondered that, too. But you don't need an eye for a camera. The lens provides that. They must have another purpose."

"Maybe it's research work on robotic eyes?" Ariel suggested. "For people who have bad eyesight? I read about some sort of equipment that helps blind people see to some degree."

"I'm not prepared to think it's just a coincidence," I said slowly, "that there are five hologram eyes and five rucksacks and five passports."

"And the five red pins on the five cities, with the 'Z' numbers?" Zak added.

That reminded me of the list of names and numbers in the file. I asked the others if anyone knew what they meant. Nobody did. "One list mentioned Zenith," I said. "Zenith plus a number up to five."

"But why have they all got work coveralls, tools and military-style rations?" Sophie asked after a pause. "Are members of the Zenith team going on some sort of field exercise, like the army?"

"That's what I was thinking," I replied. "I've just discovered that the final level of training involves close quarters combat."

"Maybe they're going to practice some kind of survival tactics?" Zak asked.

"Maybe." I would mention all this to Boges too, next time we talked. He might have some more ideas.

"Who owned the passports?" Sophie asked.

"One of them belonged to someone called Georgia Montgomery," I said.

"Georgia Montgomery?" Sophie's eyes widened. "She used to help train my group, I mean before I was kicked out. She was way more advanced than most of us. The others used to call her Spidergirl."

An image flashed in my mind, something I'd seen when I was hiding above the training arena hidden deep within the mountain—the memory of a girl I'd seen practically *running* up the walls that arched over the huge arena. "I think I've seen her! She was climbing the wall in the training area."

"She was amazing," said Sophie. "She sure

deserved her nickname." She frowned. "What other names did you see?"

"I didn't have time to look at any of the others. Georgia Montgomery's was the only one I saw."

Sophie frowned, "So what's with the little pellets in the blister packs in the locked cupboard?"

There was a silence.

"I wonder . . ." Ariel began to say.

"Go on," urged Zak.

"Well, I've seen movies where people get injected with tracking devices. What if it's something like that?"

"I can speak from personal experience and tell you that's entirely possible," I grimaced, thinking of the bug Oriana had once put in my shoulder.

"Or maybe it's even some kind of medicine. Perhaps the Biosurge stuff could be the implant that the Zenith team get. But rather than inject it, for some reason it has to be surgically implanted," Sophie said.

"Ryan and I wondered if the wound on their arms was caused by the implant," I said. "Biosurge could be the special performance-enhancing mixture."

"But then why all the secrecy and the pressure? We were told it was just a ritual; sounds like they're telling all kinds of lies about it. And look at the trouble we got in for rejecting it. I don't think we can believe anything Hamish or Damien says about it. It's all so creepy," Zak said.

Zak was right. It was creepy. As creepy as holographic eyes.

8:36 am

I had even more frightening news to share. Taking a deep breath, I described how I'd had to hide when I heard Damien and Hamish coming along through the tunnels. "And then I realized," I continued, "that Damien and Hamish were taking food supplies to people down there."

"The missing kids?" Sophie asked.

"That's my guess. I was following them, but I had to make a break for it when I had the chance."

"We must get them out of there," said Ariel, shuddering. "I can't imagine how horrible it must be, being locked up in some dungeon underneath the island."

"You bet we'll get them out," said Zak. "Cal, we have to go back down there and find out exactly where they're being held."

"Why do you think he's locked them up?" I asked. "It seems like such a drastic thing for him to do."

"I think it's pretty clear," said Zak. "The reason Ariel and I ran away from the resort was because we didn't want the implant. I think the others that he's locked up are in the same boat as we were—they've refused to have the implants. And for some reason, they're not allowed to just go home like everyone else. Maybe they know too much or something?"

"I wonder what that 'something' is," I said slowly. "Or . . ."

"Or—what?" Sophie asked, her blue eyes clouded with concern.

I shrugged. "Wish I knew."

"What about the prisoner on Delta 11?" asked Sophie. "We can't forget him."

"I wonder who he is?" Ariel said. "Who could Damien hate, or fear, so much that he'd put them in solitary confinement on a rock?" She sighed.

"That's been bothering me too," I replied.

"Perhaps it's one of the counselors?" Zak offered. "Someone who found out what he'd done to some of the kids, or didn't like whatever it is he's doing?"

"Well, whoever he is, we'll get him too," I promised. I sounded confident, but I sure wasn't feeling it. "And I overheard Damien say that he'd only have to bring food for whoever is locked up down there for another sixty days," I continued. "And that's not all he said. He said the first five were ready and the others would be soon."

"He *must* have been talking about the kids he's got locked up," said Ariel. "He's obviously got a deadline in mind, but why? What's he doing with these kids?"

I shook my head in frustration. I didn't like the sound of it at all.

8:58 am

I took the solar charger from my backpack and went outside into a clearing where the sun shone to charge my two phones. As I stretched in the warm sun for a moment and looked around at the lush jungle, I struggled to match up the idea of this tropical paradise with the reality of the increasingly sinister goings-on. But it was the reality that we had to face now.

"OK, Cal," Zak said, as I crawled back inside. "What's our next move?"

"I want to go back down into the tunnels and try the master key on other doors down there," I said. "Those prisoners are somewhere in that maze. I think I got pretty close to where they are being held before I had to get out." I paused. "There's something else you all need to know, that's going to make our lives a whole lot more dangerous." I told them about Damien's plan to lie about an infection so that everyone in the resort would be after us.

"No one's ever found this cave so far," said Zak, but I could see that he was worried.

"Ideally, we need another place," I said.

"There's always the bolt-hole near the cave," suggested Ariel. "Although it's pretty small."

"Maybe. But I'm thinking we need somewhere they'd never think to search. Plus we don't know how many people we're going to end up with. The bolt-hole won't hold us all." I had no idea if the master key would work, but if it did, where were we going to hide these kids and how were we going to get them and the Delta 11 prisoner off the island safely?

One thing at a time, I remembered Dad saying. Don't get overwhelmed by a big job. Just do the next sensible thing. I forced myself to slow down and think clearly. The next sensible thing was to get back inside the mountain and find the prisoners down there. We could start on that right away.

In the short silence that followed, Sophie stood, walked to the back of the cave, bending her head under the low ceiling near the wall, then turned and came back, planting herself in front of us. "We've got to tell my father about this. This is getting way out of control. Damien is a criminal. Who knows what else he's up to? We don't know what he's doing with the Zenith team, or the kids who've gone missing."

"Sophie's right," I said. "We've gotta tell BB."

"But tell him what?" asked Zak. "What if they launch a full-scale invasion of the island? Anything could happen. When we were in trouble for refusing the implant, Damien lost his temper with us and said that he'd go to any lengths if somebody got in his way. We can't take any risks, not until we've found the prisoners. He might hurt them."

"You're right," Ariel agreed. "We can't risk endangering anyone."

I thought about what they were saying. "I understand what you mean, but BB's not stupid. Surely he'd be able to figure out something that wouldn't alert Damien and his people. I'm going to make contact tonight."

"Good," said Sophie. "I need to talk to him, too. I want to put things right between us. I feel like I can't wait any longer to make it up with him . . ."

Her voice petered out.

"Hey," I said, putting my hand on her shoulder. "It'll be OK, all right? He'll be so happy to hear from you, I'm sure everything else will be forgotten."

Sophie's blue eyes looked hard into mine. "I hope you're right, Cal," she said finally.

Shadow Island Jungle

11:49 am

I stepped outside to bring the solar charger and the phones back inside. The tropical rainforest was teeming with life as birds flitted wildly overhead. I was about to turn back to the cave when a movement in the jungle undergrowth made me freeze. Coming towards me, its head rearing up from the rest of its body, was a spython, its beady eyes staring straight at me as I tried to shrink back into the foliage. If I dealt with it in some direct way and someone was watching the monitor screens back at the compound, I would be identified right away. Or at least, Ryan would. Which would be just as bad. I called out to Zak behind me in the cave. "Zak! How good a shot are you?"

Within seconds, both of the Katzes were beside me, hidden in the leaves, their arrows drawn right back against their taut bows.

"He's pretty good," said Ariel. "You want us to take out that spython?"

I didn't even have time to answer. Zak fired first. The twang and rush of his arrow whooshed past me, hitting the head of the spython. The head jerked back, twisting. It looked as if Zak's shot had gone straight through its right "eye." Ariel fired second, her arrow pinning the head section to the ground. The spython's body contorted uselessly, thrashing in the undergrowth, the segments of its body no longer moving together. With its cameras disabled and its head wedged tight to the ground by Ariel's arrow, this spy wouldn't be sending any more information back to headquarters. It certainly wouldn't be reassembling, like the last one we'd encountered in the jungle. "Hey! Great shots, both of you!"

"Ariel is better than me," said her brother, grinning. They shook hands and congratulated each other.

"So what do we do with it?" Zak said.

"We can't leave it here, it might lead them straight to us," I said. "We need to get rid of it."

"That sounds like a job for me," Ariel said. She handed her bow to Zak as she pulled the arrows out of the spython's head. She heaved the robot over her shoulder. "I'll take this over to the other side of the island, lead them on a wild goose chase for us," she laughed, as she walked off into the jungle.

I followed Zak back inside, wriggling in through the leaves surrounding the hidden cave's entrance, folding the solar charger away and carefully zipping up the secure phone inside my jacket. I was hugely impressed by Ariel's and

Zak's talents, and was very glad they were on my team.

3:54 pm

Boges finally called me back later that afternoon as I lay outside getting some fresh air, hidden by a large tree. "Man, that file you emailed me—the Mordred key? I opened it on one of my throw-out rebuilt laptops, in case it melted my system or something. And I'm telling you, dude, I don't like the look of it at all."

"Tell me!" I urged. "What is it? We need to know."

"I'd tell you if I could. It's heavily encrypted. I've never seen script like it before. I mean that. I've already talked with SI-6 about it. They're scratching their heads, too. They've sent the file to their top IT cipher department to see if they can crack it. I found a few helpful things, though. Not promising anything at this stage, but I might be able to hack into Damien's email."

"That might help with the encrypted file," I said doubtfully. "I'd really like to know what it's all about."

"Relax, Cal. One of the greatest minds in history is working on it."

"You, Boges?"

"That would be correct, dude."

"Ryan's about to move to the next level—the

Zenith team. And I've found out that this top-level group learn close quarters combat skills. But what for?"

"Good question," said Boges.

I went on to tell him about everything I'd seen in the lab.

Boges was silent for a while. "Don't know what that's all about," he finally said. "What were the six letters at the top of that paper?"

"MAC-UID," I quoted.

"Well, now you're talking," said Boges. "Finally something I understand. MAC is short for Media Access Control, and that might explain some of the names and numbers, too. The Media Access Control is an electronic address allocated to every electronic device. They all have a unique ID, and that's what UID means."

"So those strings of names and numbers are the identifying markers for things like cell phones and computers? That sort of thing?"

"Right. You got it," Boges said.

"And I took one of the Biosurge pellets," I said. "We need to get it analyzed, find out what these so-called natural vitamins are all about."

"I know a bloke in the chemistry department at the university," said Boges. "I could ask him to run it through a chemical analysis and find out what's actually in it."

"I have to get it to you first," I said. "I don't really know how long I'm going to be on the island." I thought about the winking cubes. "I heard Damien say something about the cubes, that they'd moved. He called them modbots."

"Did you say modbots?" Boges asked.

"That's right," I said.

"Do you know what that means?" Boges said.

"No, Boges, but I'll bet you do."

"It's short for 'modular robots,'" said Boges. "A lot of work's being done in that area at the moment. Modbots are a bit like a kid's toy blocks, but with brains. They come in different shapes and sizes and can be grouped together in different formations."

I told him about the heavy, rover-type vehicle that I'd bumped into, and asked him about the screen on the dashboard.

"That sounds like the sort of big robotic machine they use in mining," said Boges. "Could explain how some of the tunnels were made. The screen might have radar capability. Miners use it to see minerals behind a rock face."

"The screen did show me the rock face in front of the machine, but some of the pixels were moving. What do you make of that, Boges? Oh man, and I forgot to tell you about the eyes! There were five, all different colors . . . hey, Boges? Are you still there?"

"Hey . . . Cal. Hello? You there? . . . breaking up."

"That's not me," I said. "There's been some earthquakes happening on the island."

"Cal—be careful . . . could be . . . volcano . . ."

"We'd kinda worked that out, Boges."

"I think . . . but you don't need to . . . out of there . . . don't panic, volcanoes sometimes behave like that for months before they finally . . ."

Then I lost him completely as the line went dead. "There's some serious atmospheric interference happening," I explained to the others as I came back inside the cave.

I pulled out the brochure from the lab that I'd shoved in my pocket. "Have a look at this." The others crowded around to see.

Sophie read aloud over my shoulder, "'Thoroughgood Robotics—automated mining capabilities. Search and rescue applications over multiple terrains.' What does that mean?"

On the cover of the brochure was the name of the author—Dr. Jeffrey Thoroughgood, PhD.

"I've heard of him," said Sophie. "He's Damien's brother. Mrs. Clayton told me he's an amazing robotics designer and engineer. He's practically a billionaire. He donated this place— gave away this whole island—so that kids could have somewhere to chill out for a while."

"That would explain why I overheard Hamish saying that Jeffrey would be pleased with the modbots. Maybe he was talking about some kind of experiment that Jeffrey was working on?"

I continued reading aloud, "'Thoroughgood Robotics supplies state-of-the-art radar-equipped rovers for mining that can also be used to locate and dig out people trapped in disaster areas. Thoroughgood Robotics can supply modular robotic systems for any terrain which will help in search and rescue operations across many situations—from earthquake searches to mining accidents. Our designs can assist in digging underneath and photographing under collapsed buildings or caved-in mine systems. The uses to which our flexible robotic systems can be put are only limited by the human imagination. You've got a problem? Thoroughgood Robotics multi-application modular robots offer you the solution!'"

"So where is he when we need him?" joked Zak. "Maybe he could help us with a few solutions!"

"Sophie's dad told me that he's been sick recently, and that's why Damien has been running the place," I said.

"Well, I guess those camera snakes would be helpful after an earthquake," Zak said. "You can imagine them sliding into crevices and finding people trapped under rubble and sending back information so rescuers could get to them quickly."

"I bumped into one of his mining machines just near the laboratory," I said. "That could explain why there are so many tunnels down there. Looks like Jeffrey has been using his improved automated digging and cutting implements to create more of those tunnels under the mountain. And it explains the spythons, too. Jeffrey must have been using Shadow Island like a field laboratory, digging tunnels with his robot digger and testing his search and rescue pythons."

"They're not doing search and rescue now," Ariel said. "They're *spying*—sending back information to whoever is monitoring the security screens in Damien's office."

"Hamish," I said, thinking of the burly, bristle-headed guy with the broad shoulders and the piercing gray eyes. "He's his second-in-command."

"Hamish and Damien served in the army together," said Ariel. "Hamish told me ages ago that he owes his life to Damien."

"No wonder they're so tight," I said.

I flipped through the rest of the brochure. "Well, there's nothing in here about holographic eyes."

11:00 pm

I tried calling SI-6 using the secure satellite phone that BB had given me. I had no luck. Bad weather, earthquakes—whatever was preventing the connection, the result was the same.

We were on our own.

DAY 38

53 days to go . . .

Katz Cave

6:35 am

With just a hint of pink light along the horizon, I crept out of the cave to have a look at the volcano. I could see a thin line of smoke snaking up into the sky. All appeared still. The birds didn't seem worried by it. They were as noisy as ever—screeching parrots and other tuneful songsters created a musical racket in the treetops as heavy drops of water splashed down from the forest cloud above.

Maybe there wasn't anything to worry about after all. The earthquakes had stopped in the last few days and there was no other sign that anything else was going to happen up at the volcano's summit.

Over the last week, Ryan had kept me informed about comings and goings at the resort, so I knew that Damien had succeeded in convincing everyone that the runaways were sick and needed urgent attention. I'd even heard some of them calling out to us as they combed the island, begging us to come in for treatment. There was no point trying to convince them that Damien was lying—even if we could persuade them, we'd only be endangering them further. So we hid and we waited.

Every day we could hear search parties being organized over the loudspeakers. From the snatches we heard, it seemed that the counselors were doing most of the searching, with only a handful of resort kids rostered on at any one time.

So he gets them to help search, but does it in shifts so they can still have fun and not suspect too much. That's clever, makes sure they don't get sick of it all and want to leave, I thought.

The searchers had been surprisingly persistent, though. We'd had no choice but to lie low and wait for their zealousness to wear off.

We focused our energies on figuring out our next move and trying to fix the satellite phone, which had stopped working several days before. In between his training sessions and reward excursions, Ryan had managed to find some tools in a resort storeroom and Zak had been tinkering with it since. I moaned about the broken phone, but Zak seemed glad to have something to occupy his time.

Back inside the cave, I squatted on one of the cartons as the rescue plans I'd been thinking about crystallized in my mind.

"OK," I said, looking at Zak and Ariel who were opening cans of baked beans and boxes of cookies for breakfast. Sophie had just come back from the creek where we washed when we were sure it was safe from spying eyes, and pulled up a crate to join us.

"I think we need to take a chance out in the jungle. It seems like maybe the searchers are getting a bit halfhearted now. I think it's best if Zak and I go out to Delta 11. We don't know what state that prisoner might be in. We need to get him out of that prison and off the outcrop."

"So we need to figure out how to get the key," Zak said. "And then get ourselves out to Delta 11?"

Two problems. My mind raced to solve them. One at a time, I reminded myself.

"The key to Delta 11 is in Damien's office. I saw it there. We'll have to risk another trip into the resort for the key or get Ryan to sneak back in. But in the meantime, we'll talk to the prisoner and find out how he's doing. BB might have to fly in medical supplies if necessary. As for getting over there, we'll need to 'borrow' the little boat with the outboard. But it won't be easy doing that without getting caught. Especially now."

"I've got a better idea," said Zak. "Come with me."

Curious, I followed Zak out of the cave and some distance away, through thick jungle to a very narrow crevasse in the rock, so narrow that he could barely squeeze through. But soon he was backing out, hauling something. I hurried over to give him a hand and as it came out, I soon realized what it was—a wide, flat construction, like wooden flooring, securely held together by strong ropes.

"A raft! Awesome!"

"We made it ages ago," Zak explained. "We've even tried to launch it a couple of times, but without the right tools to make oars, it was too hard to row."

"We could use the oars from the outboard," I said excitedly. "Damien and Hamish would notice the boat missing, but I think we can get away with taking the oars."

"We'll all need to help get it down to the shoreline and then hide it there so we're ready to go over to the outcrop," Zak said.

We hauled the raft, mostly on its edge, through the undergrowth and vines of Shadow Island. We used the strong rope attached to the raft to drag it through cleared areas, carrying it in other places.

"Thank goodness it's mostly downhill," puffed Sophie as we paused for a rest.

"I hope we're not making too much noise," I said. "What we need is one of those tropical downpours."

As if by magic, thunder rumbled overhead and a tropical rainstorm exploded around us, the rain falling straight down, heavy and loud. Despite everything, it made me laugh.

"Hey, Cal! You never told us you were a rainmaker!" Sophie grinned.

The hammering rain gave us just the cover we needed as we bullied and shoved, pushed and lifted the large raft all the way down to the shoreline. We emerged from the undergrowth, drenched and dripping with sweat and rain. The southern tip of the island hid us from the large mooring cavern around the corner and the resort buildings farther north, but we'd still have to be vigilant: there were counselors searching everywhere.

"It'd be best to hide it down here," Zak said, looking around for a suitable place. There really wasn't anywhere to conceal it along the rocky coastline. I looked around, wondering if we'd have to haul the raft back up into the undergrowth somewhere, when I noticed a long piece of driftwood beyond the rocks, wallowing in the water. It was wedged fast between two jagged rocks and had been there so long that it was covered in dozens of barnacles and lumpy seaweed.

"Let's hide it in plain sight," I said. "We can tie one end of the rope tight around this jammed log and let the raft drift out beyond the rocks. No one will notice it."

I secured the rope with the strong double clove hitch that my father had taught me, and together we managed to wrangle the raft out beyond the surrounding jagged rocks in the water. It drifted lazily on the swell and when I went back to check the rope around the log, seaweed had already drifted around it so that it was almost invisible. I was satisfied with our plan.

Shadow Island Jungle

8:42 am

The rain had stopped as suddenly as it began and we rested for a while, dozing in the undergrowth. Over the still air, the sound of voices began to drift towards us.

"More search parties," sighed Sophie. We

silently looked at each other and nodded. Time to go. We fell into single file as Ariel led us back to our hide-out. No one spoke as we crept along like jungle ninjas.

Once we were safely back in the cave, I shared the rest of my plan with the others. "Tomorrow, when everyone is spread out on the mountain looking for us again, we'll sneak inside and try to find the prisoners locked up down there. We'll go to the cave where the submersible and the motorboat are moored so Zak and I can take the oars from the motorboat. The search parties should miss us because you guys will be inside the mountain, and Zak and I will be on the raft headed for Delta 11. Sophie and Ariel, you two take the master key and search for those prisoners. I know you both have some idea of the layout inside the mountain and Sophie, you remember roughly where you were held?"

She nodded.

"We know there are at least two tunnels that open onto the big mooring cave, including the one that runs past the underground dining room—search that one first. If we're lucky, there may be other rooms down there that we missed before. That master key is our most precious possession. Whatever you do, don't let them find that. Swallow it if you have to!"

"Hopefully it won't come to that!" Sophie smiled.

"Don't worry," said Ariel. "We won't let you down. Promise."

DAY 39

52 days to go . . .

9:02 am

We were ready. From the resort, we could hear the loudspeakers organizing that day's search and rescue operation. What a load of bull, I thought. Damien was keeping up the pretense that the runaways were "sick" and that he was organizing some sort of mercy operation, and all along he was simply plotting to capture them.

We all hurried south, on our way to the mooring cave and its opening into the tunnels of the mountain. No matter how many times I'd made this crazy scramble across the rocks, it still seemed hard and made me a bit fearful.

It was Sophie's turn to wear the stinger suit, but fortunately, the sea wasn't too wild around the opening of the cave and we were all able to get inside without getting drenched.

"Good luck, girls," I said to Sophie and Ariel, and Zak gave his sister a quick hug. We watched them vanish into the darkness of the tunnel opposite.

"I'm going to take a look at that boat," Zak said, pointing to the submersible. "You never know, maybe we can use it to leave when we've gotten everyone together."

"I'll go for the oars." I crept towards the motorboat that was bobbing on its rope. I jumped down and grabbed the oars, steadying the little boat with my legs, and then lifting the oars out onto the ledge.

Zak came back shaking his head. "No go," he sighed, "there's a serious electronic padlock on the controls; we'd need the code."

"Shoot, that's a pity. Good thinking, though. Let's get going," I said. I'd never noticed any security cameras underground, but I wasn't taking any chances and the quicker we were out of there, the better.

We hurried back to the entrance of the cave. It was difficult negotiating the slippery rocks while holding the oars as well, but with each other's help, we made it back to retrieve the raft which had become wedged between rocks. It took all of our strength to free it, but at last we were able to jump on, push away from the rocks and steer with the oars. Once past the rocks, we settled into a steady rhythm and even found a helpful current that seemed to run between the coast and the outcrop.

It was a beautiful morning and I just hoped that nobody was looking down along this coastline from higher up on the mountain because we'd be spotted for sure. The raft was awkward to manage, but it didn't take us too long to reach the dangerous, jagged rock formations that almost surrounded the Delta 11 outcrop like a semicircle of glistening black teeth.

I managed to lash the raft around the needle-like formation of volcanic rock not far from the shoreline, and with the oars held high out of the water, we pushed against the surging water, wading onto the sloping stony beach.

We stowed the oars safely out of sight and hunkering down, crept towards the bunker. In the daylight, the cement bunker seemed even more desolate as it squatted on the rocks of the outcrop, with only the narrow gun slits allowing in any light. I pointed out the barred window, high up the stone wall, to Zak.

I called out, "Hey! I've come back. I promised to help you, remember?"

For a few moments all we could hear was the sound of the breakers on the ocean side of the outcrop, smashing against the rocks. I moved closer to be right under the barred window. "Are you there?" I called, as Zak stepped up beside me.

This time, something moved near the bars and a pale face appeared. All we could see were some eyes and a nose, the rest of the face was obscured by a bushy moustache and beard.

"Help me! Get me out of here . . . please." His voice was croaky and frail.

"Is there any way we can get in to you?" I called.

"Only the man who brings food has a key."

Zak and I looked at each other.

"Who are you?" I asked.

There was a long silence.

"I'm not sure. I think they're putting something in my food and water. But I have to eat or I'll starve. Although maybe that's better than rotting in here."

Another silence.

"Can you tell us who locked you up?"

"I can't remember."

"Or why they did it?"

A long pause. "They wanted something— something that was mine."

I saw him shake his bushy head. "It's no use. I can't remember anything. I just sit around all day and night. I feel like I'm losing my mind."

"Listen," I said, "we're going to get the key,

and we're going to get you out."

I wasn't exactly sure how we were going to manage that, but I had to give this man some hope.

"Who are you?" the man asked, and already I could tell his voice was stronger than before.

"My name is Cal," I said, "and this is my friend Zak. We've been staying on Shadow Island for a while. I promise we'll be back as soon as we get the key. Now, there's something you can do."

"Me? I can't do anything."

I understood his despair and depression. Anyone would feel hopeless in his situation. But I also knew from my own experience that there was something he *could* do to help himself.

"Start exercising. Please. I know you're probably really weak. But just try with one push up. And the next day, try two. Or three?"

There was a long silence and I thought he was ignoring my suggestion. Finally the cracked voice spoke again. "I'll try anything. Just get me out!"

"We'll do our best," I said, "and in the meantime, start gaining your strength back. Every little bit will help."

"I'm so weak . . . but, I will try," he paused. "I used to be someone before—someone important. I'll never find myself again if I don't get away from this place."

It was amazing to hear the change in his voice already. Now his voice had a little bit of life in it. I guess he'd been feeling that he would never escape from this desolate prison.

"We'll return soon," I repeated. "I'm not too sure when, but we'll be back."

Zak and I hurried away, picked up the oars and untethered the raft. The heat was building up now, and we had no shelter as we plied the oars towards Shadow Island. Over the water, we could hear the calls of the searchers and I hoped it wouldn't even occur to them to look out to sea. As we approached the shoreline of Shadow Island, I thought also about Sophie and Ariel. I hoped like crazy they were OK.

10:33 am

It turned out to be very difficult to land the raft against the protruding rocks sticking out in the violent surf. It took several attempts and we were exhausted before we finally were able to lash the raft against the huge jammed log. All the time, I was scanning the undergrowth, worried that at any moment a group of searchers might break through the foliage near the shoreline and spot us, or look down from a higher vantage point and see us floundering around in the water and raise the alarm.

But finally we had the job done. After crawling back over the rocks to return the oars, we collapsed in a sheltered spot near the shoreline and rested for a while. Then we were able to start making our way back up the mountain. We nearly got caught as we headed inland, aiming for our hidden cave. A couple of counselors from the resort would have walked straight into us, except for the fact that they stopped to look at something. That gave us time to melt back into the undergrowth and wait until they'd walked off together.

"That was close," whispered Zak.

"Too close. We have to be extra careful from now on."

The girls still hadn't returned by nightfall and I was getting really worried. So was Zak. He kept creeping out of the cave to stand and listen, but all we could hear were the distant calls of the searchers.

"Do you think they've been caught?" he asked.

"I just don't know. Let's hope not," I replied.

11:01 pm

When it was time to try calling BB again, the girls still hadn't reappeared. I was really worried now. If they didn't come back soon, I knew we'd have to go searching for them.

"Here goes," I said to Zak, "let's hope it's working now." I radioed SI-6. The signal was strong and clear! "Good work, Zak!" I whispered to him.

"Night hawk?" the phone crackled.

"Condor?" I replied to confirm my identity.

"Great to hear from you, Cal!"

"Paddy?" I said, recognizing his voice.

"At your service," he replied.

"I really need to talk to BB."

"BB's not available at the moment. Some security emergency has come up. I don't know what it is, but it's a big deal. But I'm here and I'm listening. I can pass anything on to him," Paddy said.

"OK, then. Well, you guys know that things are getting very complicated," I said.

"Go on."

Paddy listened while I gave him a quick rundown, particularly about Damien locking up people underground and the prisoner on the outcrop. "And there's a big search on for us. We're under a lot of pressure. We need help to get off the island. We have a frail man who might need medical attention and I don't know how the other prisoners are doing."

"I don't like the sound of this," said Paddy. "I'll let BB know all of this information and we'll figure out what to do."

We agreed that I'd stay on the island until we could figure out what Damien was up to and rescue the prisoners ready for evacuation. Paddy reassured me that he'd send in the cavalry immediately if I said the word.

"If possible, I imagine you don't want any obvious landings on the island?" he said.

"No," I said, with relief.

"Leave it with me. I'll talk to BB about it and once we decide on our next move, we'll contact you. OK? Meanwhile we'll keep working on the Mordred file and let you know if we manage to crack the encryption. For the time being, just stay out of trouble."

"I'll do my best," I promised. I ended the call, and felt some of the anxiety and concern I'd been feeling lift, knowing that SI-6 were in the loop.

But I was still restless and edgy, and so was Zak. We just couldn't settle and I knew he was as concerned as I was—maybe even more so—about Ariel and Sophie.

Eventually, I left Zak dozing and started climbing down through the jungle, thinking that I would start my search for them now, despite the dark night. I went a little way, using the narrow beam of light from my flashlight. But I had to give up—it was just too dangerous. I almost walked into a Gympie Gympie tree, saved only by some instinct that made me flash the beam of light upward. I reeled back in shock. Another step and I'd have walked straight into the toxic leaves. I needed to stay strong and healthy if I was going to be of any help to anyone. Reluctantly, I turned back.

DAY 40

51 days to go . . .

Early the next morning, after a restless few hours trying to sleep, we were determined to go looking for Sophie and Ariel. Zak brought his bow and arrows, and as we stepped out into the early morning mist, the volcano suddenly growled and the earth trembled under our feet. This time it was a long quake, more violent than previous ones. Birds squawked and flapped from the trees, wheeling around before they settled again. What would happen to us all on Shadow Island if the volcano finally decided to blow? I didn't like to think about it.

As the shaking finished, we got up from crouching under the trees, but I immediately pushed Zak straight back down again. "Shhh! Someone's coming!"

Someone was moving very stealthily towards us—were they aiming for the cave? I peered through the jungle undergrowth, trying to get a look at whoever was approaching. I watched as Zak soundlessly took out an arrow and readied his bow to fire. I was too scared to breathe. I couldn't believe Damien had already started a search for us at this hour. The man was truly relentless.

The two figures ahead of me froze in their tracks. I could barely recognize them, they were so filthy. When I saw who it was, I jumped up, hauling Zak with me.

"Cal! Zak! It's us. Don't shoot!" they whispered as loudly as they could.

"Sophie! Ariel! Thank goodness you're safe. You nearly frightened me out of my skin! I thought the searchers were about to find us," I exclaimed.

I took a closer look at them. "But where have you been? And *what* have you been doing? You look terrible!"

"Thanks a lot. You do know how to flatter a girl. Let us wash up a bit and I'll tell you everything," Sophie promised. "And please, food! We need breakfast!"

"Dinner and lunch as well," said Ariel. "I'm starving!"

The girls cleaned themselves up at the creek, while Zak and I pulled out some of our rapidly dwindling food supplies. The girls returned, wearing their washed, damp clothes. Both girls wolfed down several granola bars.

"OK," Sophie said after swallowing another handful of dried fruit. "We went into the tunnel you'd told us about, and we looked everywhere. We found all sorts of tunnels and dead ends. It's a labyrinth down there." She pulled the wrapping off another granola bar and bit it in half before continuing.

"We found that laboratory you told us about and checked through the glass window in the door to make sure that there were no spythons around, but it was all clear."

The stupid thing must have moved, I thought, looking around anxiously.

"Then we went inside and had a look. Those modbots that you told us about? They were piled up into some sort of tower."

I frowned. "A tower? I wonder what that's for? They were just a big pile of blocks when I saw them."

"Well, they were in this big tower as if they'd been deliberately stacked," Ariel continued, "but then they collapsed."

Sophie shrugged. "We didn't touch them. They just fell over. We were looking at those rucksacks you told us about, and then out of nowhere the modbots moved and gave us a real fright."

"They moved?"

Both Sophie and Ariel nodded vigorously. "Two of them climbed on top of two other ones."

Zak turned his puzzled face to me, as his sister continued speaking.

"Anyway, we realized that someone must have given them a signal and that they might be close by, so we bolted out of there. We didn't get to see the hologram eyes."

"We kept searching up and down the tunnels," Sophie said, taking over the story as Ariel demolished a chocolate bar.

"Any sign of the prisoners?" I asked.

Sophie and Ariel looked at each other.

"We think we *might* have made some sort of contact with them," Sophie said.

"We weren't sure," Ariel said, taking over. "We came up against this huge iron door and we tried the key in it. But we could see that the lock was some old convict-era job." She searched around in one of the pockets of her jacket.

"What makes you think they're locked up behind that door?" I asked.

"We tapped on it and we think someone tapped back on the other side," said Ariel.

"We tried calling out, but couldn't shout loud enough for our voices to penetrate the iron door without risking someone else in the tunnels hearing us," Sophie added. "It was very frustrating. I don't know how we're going to get them out of there—if that's where they are. It really is like a prison."

I thought of the heavy door of the bunker on Delta 11. "At least we know where the prisoners might be," I said, feeling a little hopeful. "Now it's just a matter of finding that key. Hamish or Damien must keep it somewhere handy—they must bring them food at least every few days."

Maybe Hamish had that key, I thought. I hadn't seen an old-fashioned key hanging on the key rack in Damien's office. I'm sure I would have remembered a key like that.

"But we did find something else amazing!" said Sophie. "At the end of another tunnel we'd been searching, hoping to find another way to get to the prisoners, I tripped and fell against some stacked wood. A couple of huge beams came loose and some rubble fell along the tunnel. That set off a kind of mini rockfall. After I got over the shock—we saw what had happened. The wood had been hiding an old door, and when the beams fell against it, they pushed it open a little. The hinges were rusted so we were able to squeeze through."

"So what was beyond the door?" I asked. "The suspense is killing me!"

Ariel rolled her eyes. "Big surprise, another tunnel! This one was *really* filthy. Totally smothered in dust. There were even *bones* down there—we didn't stop to look at them too long—and the tunnel was almost blocked with massive cobwebs. Looked like they'd been collecting dust for a century. It was like walking through rotting clotheslines, with ancient, dirty cobwebs sticking to our faces and arms!"

Sophie interrupted, unable to wait for Ariel to continue. "We started exploring and realized we were in a really long tunnel that went uphill. It took us ages, fighting our way through those disgusting cobwebs, but finally we came to some steps. The dust was half a foot thick on them. A crack of light was showing along the length of a stone slab. After a lot of heaving and grunting, the two of us were able to push it over, and—guess where we were?"

I shook my head. "No idea. Tell us!"

"In the cemetery! The stone slab was the wall of a grave—Simeon Fincher, whoever he was," Sophie said.

"Some poor convict who died and was buried a long way from home," said Ariel. "And we were very, *very* relieved to find that there was no trace of poor Simeon. So the tunnel system is connected all the way to the cemetery—only a stone's throw away from the resort fence! How cool is that?"

"But we had to go back," Sophie took up the story again. "We couldn't risk being spotted in the cemetery. That old tunnel was almost as revolting on the way back, although we were already wearing half of the cobwebs. But eventually we got back to the broken door. By then we were exhausted and had a rest, hidden behind the fallen woodpile. We must have fallen asleep, but when we woke up, we couldn't get out of there fast enough." Sophie shuddered. "I hope I never have to go through anything like that tunnel again. It was totally gross!"

"Perfect!" I said. "It sounds perfect."

Sophie and Ariel swung on me, eyes wide. "What do you mean 'perfect?' Haven't you been listening?"

"Absolutely," I said. "From what you say, no one has been in that tunnel for a hundred years. No wonder it's filled with dust and cobwebs. Which means Damien, Hamish and the Zenith team have no idea it's there. That's where we can go if it gets too risky to stay in the cave. And now we've got another way to get really close to the Paradise People Resort. That means we can slip through the jungle to the beach instead of having to go across the island. Hopefully the spythons will have less chance to spot us."

"Sounds like you guys got to have all the fun!" said Zak, a little enviously.

Shadow Island Jungle

10:59 pm

Leaving the others sleeping in the cave, Sophie and I stole out into the moonlight. She had finally decided that she wanted to speak to BB. I passed her the satellite phone that her father had given me and moved away from the huge rainforest tree she was leaning against to give her some privacy.

My mind wandered as I waited, thinking about how much had changed since I'd first come to Shadow Island. It seemed a lifetime ago since I'd been playing games and working out with the guys in The Edge. How could any one of us have known that my covert mission to check up on Sophie would lead to all this?

I could hear that Sophie had been successful in getting through to BB. It was a short conversation, but I heard her say, "Dad, I'm really sorry. I want to come home." Of course, I couldn't know what BB said to her, but as she returned the phone to me, she was smiling through her tears.

"Hello, BB?" I said.

"Cal!" BB replied. "I'm so grateful to you for finding Sophie, but we have to . . ."

Sophie grabbed my arm and pulled me to the ground. "Hang up!" she hissed, pointing to the left.

I killed the connection, exclaiming under my breath. We lay motionless as a couple of flashlight beams swung away down the mountain. A late-night search party had hoped to catch us unaware. Luckily, we'd avoided them this time.

I tried to call BB again later, but the static was back with a vengeance.

DAY 45

46 days to go . . .

3:32 pm

Every day, we had to take evasive action to avoid being discovered. We'd shifted some of our supplies to the cemetery end of the filthy, old forgotten tunnel as a backup, and in desperation we'd even slept there a couple of times when groups of searchers started looking for us at night. But the risk of being discovered by anyone in the tunnels, plus the disgusting and uncomfortable surroundings, made us wary of spending too much time down there.

We spent the next few days trying to put the information that we had gathered into some sort of logical pattern. When Winter and I talked, I told her I was concerned I hadn't been able to contact her.

"I've been away for a few days," she said. "Gabbi wanted to visit Perdita and meet Harriet so I organized that. And then I said to your mum, 'Why don't you come, too?' and she was really pleased with the invitation. It was exciting for Gabbi to see where the 'ghost' had been and visit Harriet's farm after hearing about how we managed to save it. You should see the place now, it looks like the Garden of Eden! She's not making a lot of money, but she's free of debt and really happy. She's joined the local theater group and seems to be having a lot more fun these days. She asked me to say hi to you, at your special flight school. Ha!"

"Good to hear," I said.

Winter's voice became more serious. "Cal, I've been thinking about that world map in the lab that you told Boges about," she said, "and what immediately came to my mind was that very first picture that was sent to your phone. That was way before we knew anything about Shadow Island."

"The one with the skull and crossbones superimposed on a map of the world?" I asked. "I agree, it has to be linked. Damien is counting the same number of days as in that message. It must all fit together somehow. But how? What do those cities have to do with Damien's plans?"

"You said there were five destinations mapped?"

"That's right," I said.

"And five very large rucksacks with rations

and passports? And sealed envelopes. Plus five hologram eyes."

"Yes. But I've no idea why."

Neither of us had an answer.

"We know that one of the passport holders, Georgia Montgomery, is most likely a member of the Zenith team. My guess is that the other four are team members, too," I said.

"But why would they all be going separately to different cities in the world? I can understand that Damien might want to reward them, but if it's team-building he's after, they would surely stay together and travel together?" Winter asked.

"If it's not about team-building," I said slowly, "then it's related to what's going on here. And we don't know anything about that yet."

"You said there were envelopes with security seals?" Winter asked.

"That's right."

"So you know what I'm thinking?" she said. "I'm thinking they're sealed orders, like commandos get—not to be opened until the mission is underway. So that no one can leak information."

"But if they are going to those major cities," I said, "there'd be absolutely no need for rations and water decontamination tablets. Why would you eat rations in Paris? It has some of the greatest restaurants in the world."

"None of it makes sense," Winter admitted. "Just like the Mordred key file."

There was a silence.

"Boges told me about the MACs and the UID names and numbers," Winter finally said. "And did you know that the other name you saw, Melehan, is Mordred's son? So that list has gotta be connected to the Mordred key in some way."

"His son? This just keeps getting stranger," I said.

"And," said Winter, continuing on another tack, "it only makes sense to take rations if you wanted to be invisible. To slip into a country and then disappear, just hunker down and hide. Like you had to, Cal, when you were living on the streets and in old houses, trying to go undetected."

"So why," I began, thinking aloud, "why would you go to a city and then disappear—with rations and sealed orders?"

"So you could wait, Cal. So you could be in position and then just wait for the command to open the orders. We've got to find out what those orders *are*, what their mission is and what on earth those creepy eyes are for!"

"I'll bet that all that information is in the Mordred file," I said. "Why else would it be so secret?" I said.

"Speaking of which, Boges is battling with that. I haven't heard from him since I got back from visiting Harriet," Winter said. "I've left messages, but he hasn't gotten back to me. He'd told me it's a full-time job just getting his head around it, let alone getting through the encryption. He said he's tried all the usual code converter programs and he's getting nowhere—total zip."

I sighed. I was starting to feel the same way. How was I going to be able to find out what the Zenith team members were going to do?

Interrupting my thoughts, Winter said, "Have you found out anything more about the missing kids?"

I told Winter how I'd followed Hamish and Damien as they took food to whoever was locked up down there, and how I'd failed to locate the prison.

"But Sophie and Ariel think they've made contact with the prisoners. I'm determined to get them out of there. But that means I need to get my hands on the key to their prison." I mentioned overhearing Damien talking, and how he'd said that in sixty days, he wouldn't have to bring food anymore.

"That's got to be related to the sixty-day countdown I saw on his computer," I said. "*And* to the message I got, but I'm no closer to figuring out who sent it to me, or why. Were they friendly? Was it a warning?"

"I don't think it means anything good, Cal."

The earth trembled again and a deep rumbling rolled across the mountain. Then just as suddenly, all was still. The quakes were coming more frequently now, I realized.

Winter's words of foreboding stayed in my mind. The sooner we all got off Shadow Island, the better.

DAY 54

37 days to go . . .

Katz Cave

8:02 am

I thought after another week that Damien would give up sending out search parties. But he didn't.

Sophie and I had carefully crept around in the early hours of the morning, and noticed with shock that he'd posted lookout stations all over the mountain, with platforms in high trees. He must be intending to have people with binoculars up there to scope out the rainforest.

We hoped we were hidden by the canopy, but the cleared areas could easily be watched and it was becoming almost impossible to move around Shadow Island. How was I going to bring a frail, possibly mentally ill man from Delta 11 into the jungle and hide him without being caught in the process? Our rescue plan seemed in jeopardy now.

We all knew that our cave hide-out was

getting dangerous, with people combing the mountainside. None of us wanted to face the idea of moving to the tunnel permanently. Worse still, whenever I tried calling SI-6, the satellite phone just gave me static.

We'd almost run out of food, too. We desperately needed supplies.

"I'm going to have to do a night raid on the food stores," I said. Zak, Ariel and Sophie all wanted to come with me. "Not a good idea," I said. "I appreciate your offers of support, guys, but this is best done by just one of us to limit the risk. I'd better avoid going across the island so I'll go down to the waterfront and cross the rocks to get in through the mooring cave. Then I can come up through the secret tunnel and get into the resort from the cemetery. The master key should get me into the stores building. I'll take our two backpacks to fill. That ought to be enough food for a few more days, and hopefully by that time BB will be in touch and we can get off the island."

Shadow Island Jungle

9:19 pm

I made my way down through the rainforest heading for the big cave on the coast. I'd texted

Ryan, telling him of my plans to steal some supplies from the stores building, asking him to be on standby in case I needed some backup.

I could hear people moving all around and went slowly and carefully to keep out of their way. From the edge of the jungle, I could just make out the raft, still safely tethered to the jammed log, moving sluggishly on the unusually still ocean. An onshore wind was flattening the surf as I broke cover and dashed across the rocks as fast as I dared. I was relieved when I finally took cover inside the mooring cave, away from the prying eyes of people above. But I still couldn't afford to take any chances—Damien or Hamish could be down here.

Underground Tunnels

9:51 pm

I stole into the main tunnel and into the darkness, discreetly switching on my flashlight, keeping it shining downward.

I could hear rumbling in the distance and wondered if someone was using the big rover machine, digging through the rock. But when I came to the widening of the tunnel at the laboratory, the huge machine was just sitting there, in exactly the same position as I'd left it, nearly three weeks before. I crept up to the door and peered cautiously through the window of the laboratory.

I frowned. The modbots sat in a square, squat pile, their lights winking. They certainly weren't built up into a tower as Sophie and Ariel had said. Curious, I used the master key to open the door, carefully looking around in case there were any spythons hanging off the light fixtures or lurking in a cupboard. The large rucksacks were still stacked in a row, leaning against the wall under the map of the world with its mysterious red strings.

I walked over to some other cupboards I hadn't had a chance to look in last time. A few were locked, but as I tried the last handle, the latch gave way and the door opened. I staggered back at the sight of more rucksacks piled up inside. There were another five. *Were these all for the Zenith team?*

I poked around in the topmost bag—the contents were just like all the others I'd seen. In a side pocket I found a handful of passports. But the corner of an envelope caught my eye. Reaching farther in, I pulled out another set of sealed orders. I had to know what they were!

I slid my finger under the seal to loosen it, but I would have to tear it to open the envelope.

Reasoning that Damien would never know it was me, I tugged hard and pulled out a thin sheet of paper.

I turned it over, holding my breath—but there was nothing. Both sides of the paper were completely blank! Where were the real orders?

I put the paper back inside the envelope and placed it where I'd found it. I quickly closed the cupboard and went over to check the 3-D eyes. I was strangely relieved to see they were still there, glowing in their light box. Nothing moved except the winking lights on the modbots. Sophie and Ariel said that they'd watched as two of the squares climbed on top of another two. I came closer to get a better look at them. They looked just as I'd remembered them—some were the creamy color of power outlets, others were black. They all had narrow slits on their surfaces and each one had blinking green lights. Hesitantly, I put out my hand to pick one up. As my hand closed around it, I jumped back in pain!

What the . . . ? Something had bitten me! I examined my hand. Two tiny puncture marks in the center of my palm already had tiny red beads of blood on them. I looked intently at the modbot cube that had attacked me. Had the cream cube "bitten" me? But how? There was nothing sharp on it, no fangs, just a bland cream surface, and

yet *something* had pierced my palm. I couldn't
see a spider or any insect that would account for
the pain in my hand.

I peered into the narrow slits that radiated
from the center, looking a little like the star-
shaped core of an apple sliced across its widest
point. I couldn't see anything in there. I put
out my hand again, carefully, as if I were about
to pick it up. Immediately, two tiny harpoons
appeared out of the slits. As I pulled my hand
away, they retracted.

Again, I curved my hand over it as if I was
going to pick it up, and again the tiny needle-
sharp harpoons appeared. This time, I noticed a
puff of smoke and felt another painful, stinging
sensation in my hand. The modbot had sprayed
me with something!

Spooked, I backed away and hurried out of the
laboratory. Somehow, the modbot had sensed my
hand moving towards it. In some strange way, it
seemed to be able to *see*—and attack.

For a few moments, I stood outside the lab,
rubbing my hand on my jacket, trying to remove
whatever had been sprayed onto my palm. The
hot, burning sensation had spread to my fingers
and thumb so that my whole hand was in pain.

To take my mind off it, I continued past the
laboratory, looking out for a turn to the right

that Ariel had said was just before the entrance to the secret tunnel. I crept along cautiously, worried that someone might appear around a corner at any moment. With my injured hand, I would find it hard to fight off an attack.

Eventually, I came to the stack of wood that Ariel and Sophie had described. Great beams of old, dry wood were piled against the wall and made it appear that the tunnel ended there. But when I shone my flashlight between the beams, I could see where the wood had been disturbed and glimpsed the door beyond.

It took me a while to lift some of the wood away because of my injured hand. I pushed the door open just enough for me to squeeze through. Once on the other side, I heaved it back into place as far as it would go. As I turned and stepped to follow the disused tunnel, I got a mouthful of the dust-laden cobwebs that Sophie and Ariel had mentioned. I pulled them off my face in disgust.

More carefully now, waving my flashlight around, I made my way along the tunnel. I could see the girls' footprints in the dust ahead of me. In some places it was nearly five inches deep. Half-buried bones lay on the sides of the rocky walls, and I saw rusty manacles and chains hanging from iron hooks. I shuddered at the thought of being chained down here and forgotten. Dust rose in clouds as I passed, and my sneakers were filthy already, as were my jeans. I sneezed and wiped my face with the back of my hand. The taste of dust was in my mouth.

The land was rising under my feet so I knew I was heading towards the cemetery, and soon enough I came to the place in the tunnel where we'd left our supplies and spent a couple of cheerless nights in hiding.

Ahead of me I could see a thin line of the dim light. I was almost there. Slowly, I pushed the heavy slab of stone over. It finally fell away, revealing the lights of the resort compound in the near distance.

Puffing and grunting with the effort, I hauled myself up and out. I took a couple of steps and then froze. One of the counselors was sitting on a nearby tombstone. Any second now she'd raise the alarm and I'd be caught.

I stood for a second or so, unsure what to do next, waiting for her to challenge me and drag "Ryan Ormond" off to Damien for being out of bounds in the cemetery.

Instead, she jumped to her feet, screaming in terror, and fled.

As I snapped out of my shock and realized what had happened, I started laughing, trying to stifle the sound with one of my filthy hands. All the tension and fear I'd been holding down for so long came out in a rush of almost hysterical laughter! But I didn't dare make too much noise.

I tried to control myself and finally straightened up, wiping away tears of laughter with my fists. I imagined the scene from her point of view: an old convict tomb opening up at night and a gray figure, draped in ragged webs, face unrecognizable with filth, crawling out. No wonder she had run away. The ghost of Simeon Fincher was on the prowl! It would have been priceless to see her trying to convince other people she wasn't just imagining things. *Good luck with that.*

But I couldn't hang around. There was a real risk she could come back with others to check it out.

Paradise People Resort

10:25 pm

Moving through the bushes near the resort, I was heartened to see that all the activity was taking place near the dormitories and recreational area to the east of the compound. Set back on the western border, the stores and generator buildings were almost deserted and in darkness, apart from dim lights over the doorways. I moved cautiously from shadow to shadow, hoping that the dust covering me would act like camouflage and keep me safe.

I sidled up to the stores building, briefly and unavoidably exposed under the light above the doorway, before the master key allowed me to slip inside and close the door behind me. Cartons of food were piled around the walls and I started grabbing the most nutritious things I could see that we wouldn't need a fire to cook—packages of nuts and dried fruits, granola bars, crispbreads and canned food. Finally, I took a powerful lamp and another strong flashlight. These would help light up the disused tunnel. I stuffed both backpacks to the brim, hauling them up over each shoulder. They were heavy, but I felt good about securing more supplies.

Shadow Island Jungle

10:58 pm

Lugging my heavy loads, I made my way back into the dark undergrowth and guided by instinct and memory, started towards the cemetery and the disused tunnel. I planned to stash most of the food stores there, only taking what we would need in the next day or two.

I was almost back at Simeon Fincher's grave

when someone slammed into my back.

"What—?"

Before I knew what was happening, both backpacks had been wrenched from my shoulders and I was sent sprawling onto the ground, face down. I couldn't believe what had just happened. I twisted around to see who it was, but already the jungle was closing around my assailant. I climbed to my feet, attempting to give chase. But in this dense undergrowth, it was too easy to lose someone in the dark, and there was no way I was going to find whoever had stolen my supplies.

I slumped in despair, feeling the energy draining out of me. After all my hard work, I'd been taken down like an idiot. I should have been on full alert. Instead I'd lost the backpacks and our much-needed supplies. My right hand, still stinging badly from the modbot attack back in the lab was now even more painful from trying to break my fall, and had collected dirt in the tiny puncture wounds on my palm.

I sat down next to the grave, trying to figure out what to do next. What were we going to eat? Slowly, I stood up. There was no point feeling sorry for myself. I'd have to make my way back to the cave and get help from the others to make a new plan.

Deciding to risk the jungle rather than try

the coastline climb over the rocks with such a sore hand, I started to move slowly through the undergrowth.

I'd been making my way through the jungle for about ten minutes when I reached the small cleared area that I remembered well from my first landing on the island, all those weeks ago. I saw something propped up against a tree that made me blink and wonder if I was seeing things. There, sitting side by side under one of the huge swamp mahogany trees, were the two full backpacks, just waiting to be picked up. I froze. What kind of trap was *this*?

I waited, listening to the silence. The occasional rustle of a small creature in the leaf litter, or the distant calling of a bird were the only sounds I could hear. I waited, crouched down. Eventually, I could wait no longer and ventured forward, swinging around in all directions, expecting an attack. All I saw were green leaves and the tangle of vines that wound through the undergrowth. I approached the backpacks as if they were booby-trapped.

I examined them thoroughly before picking the first one up. It was still full and I hauled it over my left shoulder. Then I shone the light onto the second one. It too still had its provisions, but there was something else that hadn't been there before—something I hadn't collected in the stores building. Sitting right on top, in a clear plastic box, was a USB. Gingerly, I picked it up, slipped it into my pocket and lifted the second backpack onto my right shoulder.

I swung around, hearing the sound of a branch snapping. It *had* been a trap and I was caught right in it!

But then . . . my brother suddenly emerged.

"Ryan! What are you doing here?" I asked, pleased to see him.

"I was keeping an eye on you, bro," he said. "I was waiting for you near the stores area, ready to back you up. But then I lost you for a while outside the resort. But I see you were successful." He indicated the two full backpacks.

"Someone jumped me a while ago. Did you see who it was?"

Ryan shook his head.

Facing Ryan, I failed to notice a movement in the undergrowth nearby until too late and suddenly we were both blinded by a camera flash. For a split second, the clearing lit up like midday. It caught me and Ryan, shocked and surprised, in its cold, brilliant light.

"Who's there? Who is it?" I called as someone went crashing down the hill.

The two of us stared at each other, listening

to the fading sound of the escaping photographer. The worst possible thing had happened. There was now evidence that there were two "Ryan Ormonds" on Shadow Island.

"Who was *that*?" Ryan breathed.

"Wish I knew," I said.

"Our cover is totally blown now; what will we do? I'm so close to finding out what's going on with the Zenith team, I can't believe I'll have to go on the run now. Once that photograph gets to Damien . . ." Ryan said.

"You know, I don't think that's going to happen," I said. "If you think about it, why weren't we challenged right away? Because whoever took the photograph just wants to have it—to have something just in case. It could have been one of the counselors or even one of the Paradise People. I'm half-expecting someone to make some kind of demand rather than go running to Damien with the proof of our double act. Someone set up a trap by jumping me and stealing the backpacks and then leaving them up against that tree higher up the mountain. Setting me up for a photo opportunity. And planting a USB. There is something in all this that just doesn't add up."

"Well, I hope you're right, otherwise I'm going to have a very short training session and you're going to have one more person to rescue,"

Ryan half-laughed. "I'd better get back before I'm missed," he added. "Try to stay out of the limelight from now on, would you?"

"Oh, very funny," I retorted as I shouldered the heavy backpacks and made my way back to the others.

Katz Cave

11:21 pm

Zak, Ariel and Sophie were full of questions and after I'd answered them all, I told them about the photograph that could potentially end my undercover work on Shadow Island.

Before pulling out the USB and plugging it into my phone, there was something else I wanted to say. "If Damien finds out that there have been two of us all along, he's going to feel under enormous pressure. He's not going to know how much information Ryan and I might have gathered between us. My bet is that he'll change his plans—whatever they are. Of course he might step up the search for us. But somehow, I think he's got bigger things to worry about now—like getting his Zenith team into action. He can't know how much information I might have passed on to other people. We know he's up to no good even though we don't know exactly what it is yet."

"Cal," said Sophie. "I think we need to know what's on that USB."

"Please," said Ariel.

I plugged the USB into my phone and everyone crowded around to see what was on the screen. I opened the first link and frowned. Numbered "1," it seemed to be an unremarkable diagram of the layout of a two-story building, until I looked closer. On one of the external walls was the symbol of an eye—and I immediately thought of the holographic eyes back in Jeffrey Thoroughgood's laboratory. The other oddity was a bit scarier: in another part of the building was the skull and crossbones image that we'd seen superimposed on the world map that had been sent to me.

Intensely curious, I opened the next link—number "2"—to see something very similar, although the building layout was different. But there was the eye marking a spot near an external wall and there was the skull and crossbones marking a spot inside the building. Moving more quickly, I opened numbers "3," "4" and "5." They all followed the same pattern—the image of an eye on one section of a building, always an external wall, and somewhere else, in various different positions, the skull and crossbones marked another spot on each diagram. Five different buildings, five identical markings.

The final link opened to reveal a repetition of the lists of names and numbers—all those Zeniths and Melehans and the single mention of Mordred that I'd seen in the paper file in the laboratory.

"OK," Zak asked. "Who has any ideas about these?"

"Maybe the eye marks where the security camera is on each building," Sophie suggested.

"I'm not so sure," I said. "I think they might be connected to the holographic eyes in the light box in Jeffrey Thoroughgood's laboratory."

"As for the skull and crossbones," Sophie continued, "they mark different spots in the different buildings. Are they places to be wary of? Dangerous places?"

"Like places where poison might be stored?" asked Zak. "Or weapons?" he added quietly.

I looked around at their faces—Sophie, Ariel, and Zak—all of them seeking answers. Answers I didn't have.

"Somebody wanted us to have this information," I said. "And that somebody took a photograph of me and Ryan together. It's like on the one hand they want to help, but on the other hand, they're making sure that I know that they've got something over me, something they can use against me. Like I said to Ryan, the whole incident just doesn't stack up."

"Maybe it *is* one of the Paradise People," Ariel suggested. "Or what if it's someone from the Zenith team who wants to get out?"

"I counted at least ten rucksacks," I said, "with five routes on the map, and now we have five different diagrams."

"One place each for the five Zenith teams on the list," said Sophie.

"Right," said Ariel. "Five teams . . ."

Suddenly I got it! "Five targets! Five different targets in five different cities!"

"Targets for what?" asked Zak, worry etched on his sunburned face. Silence. Another question without an answer.

"The first thing I want to do," I said, "is to get this information to SI-6—and of course, Boges. We need every brain available to be working on these questions."

"Let's draw these diagrams," suggested Sophie, "seeing as we can't print them out anywhere. We could sketch them out over against the wall, in that dust on the floor. Then we can all study them."

"Great idea," I said.

It took us a while working through each of the diagrams on the USB. I was still eager to begin searching for the keys to Damien's two prison sites, but I helped the others draw up the diagrams one after the other in the soft dusty soil.

Soon we had all five diagrams drawn out, marking the skull and crossbones and the eye symbols on each one. We stood around looking at them, trying to understand what they meant. *Observe things*, Dad would say to me, *and let what you observe tell you its story*. I walked from one to the other, observing as hard as I could. But I wasn't hearing any story, not from any of them. Five different diagrams of five different buildings. They must be located in the five cities on the map in the laboratory. But what were these buildings? What secrets did they hide?

I needed to call Boges. But given the patchy reception I was getting on my phone, I decided it was worth taking a risky trip to a high point where I could pick up a better signal to make the call.

"I've gotta go to some higher ground," I said to the others.

Shadow Island Jungle

11:28 pm

I found a sturdy tree deep in the jungle and shinned halfway up, hoping I was completely out of sight of any searchers. But, to my relief, I couldn't see anyone. The search parties, which for days had been struggling through the jungle undergrowth, had vanished. I guess they still get to sleep, I thought to myself.

As I hauled myself up, I noticed that my hand was no longer stinging from the modbot toxin. There was still slight redness running along my palm beneath my fingers and some slight itching, but the painful stinging sensation was gone.

I scanned as much as I could of the surrounding rainforest. There was no movement anywhere under the vines and trees. In fact, the place felt deserted.

Puzzled, I called Boges.

"Man, am I pleased to hear your voice!" he exclaimed, sounding instantly awake, even though I suspected I'd woken him.

"I'm pleased to talk to you too, Boges," I said, bringing him up to date with the latest happenings on Shadow Island. I told him about the modbot that had bitten me.

"That doesn't surprise me," he said, his voice serious. "They can be programmed to do pretty much anything."

"Why would Jeffrey Thoroughgood program his modbots to attack people? What's the point of locating trapped people in order to help them, and then stinging them with poison?" As I talked,

I noticed the pain in my hand throbbing again.

"Not sure. Could be just experimental."

I told him about my cover being destroyed by the photograph taken of Ryan and me together. "Someone has given us a USB," I said, "and I'm about to email its contents to you. Can you send it on to BB? That'll save me breaking cover again tonight. Actually, I'm a bit surprised that I haven't heard back from him after having to hang up on him before. And Paddy would have passed on the information by now."

Briefly, I told Boges about the discussion we'd had about the meanings of the diagrams on the USB—the layout of the buildings, the symbols of the eye and the skull and crossbones stamped in different positions.

"We think the five diagrams are targets for five teams from the Zenith group. But we don't know what they're after. Maybe the symbols mean they're planning to steal poisons from these buildings," I said.

"I'll take a good look at them," Boges promised, "and check in with SI-6 if I have a major breakthrough. And I'll try and make sense of those names and numbers on the Zenith lists."

He paused. "I think I've made some headway with the encryption of the Mordred file. I've used a cracker code and modified it so that it works much faster, and as far as I can tell, the Mordred file is a series of very elaborate instructions—which we sort of knew anyway. I've been liaising with Maxine, one of the spooks in the cyber security department of SI-6, and we both agree the first part is a very brilliant and complex penetration test which would work in about ninety-nine percent of secured systems. The rest—well, we're still working on that."

"It sounds like you're on the case, as usual, buddy," I smiled.

"But of course, dude. And as a sideline, I've managed to separate some metadata and I've even been able to hack into Damien's email. He's very security savvy and careful in what he writes—he's obviously aware of potential hackers. But there's one email contact that intrigues me. He seems to have a fiancée—in fact, he's promised to buy her a ten-million-dollar castle in Scotland as a wedding present. Some chick called Gloria Finlay. I'm trying to get into her system now. That should be easier because she probably won't have the sophisticated encryption that Damien runs his system through. So I might be able to double back into his system through hers."

"Ten million dollars? I thought it was his brother who was the billionaire," I said. "I didn't know that Damien was wealthy, too." Then something else occurred to me. "Or . . ." I began to say before Boges cut across me as we both hit on the same idea at the same time.

". . . or he's expecting to come into a lot of money very soon."

"Exactly," I said, thinking of all the movies I'd seen where highly trained thieves pull off huge jewelry heists, or robbed banks. But none of that required surgically implanted enhancing drugs, or military rations, or holographic eyes. Or any of the other mysterious items that I'd found in Jeffrey's lab. I shared my thoughts with Boges.

"Good point," he said. "Why not just use balaclavas and shotguns like a real villain?"

"Damien is planning something else, Boges. Something new. Something bad."

My last few words hung in the air.

"So, what's your next step, dude?" Boges asked.

"I've gotta get the key to Delta 11 and the key to the iron door where we think prisoners have been locked up under the mountain."

"How will you do that?" he asked.

"I'll have to break into Damien's office again. I've seen the Delta 11 key on the board there. Finding the other key is going to be trickier."

"Good luck with that, dude. I know you'll . . ." but the conversation was interrupted by a terrifying earthquake, causing the tree I was in to sway from side to side. I nearly lost my phone as I clung on, hurting my right hand against the thorny bark of the tree.

"*What was that?*" Boges asked.

"Another warning from our local volcano, I think," I said, anxiously peering through the leaves, trying to get a clear line of sight up the steep incline to the smoking hill above me. "Anyway, thanks, Boges."

"You don't have to thank me, dude. This is the kind of thing I love to sink my teeth into—metaphorically speaking, of course. Otherwise, give me pizza—with the works. OK. Over and out. And be careful with that volcano, won't you?"

He hung up and I climbed down, suddenly hankering after pizza and listening to the sharp sound of tearing leaves as they were pounded by the falling rocks and stones shaken loose by the volcano. I waited, sheltering under the tree, until the pelting stones had finished raining down. The volcano definitely was issuing a warning.

DAY 56

35 days to go . . .

9:39 pm

A frustrating couple of days had passed with no real progress. The jungle had seemed full of search parties and we had no choice but to lie low. I thought about everyone back home and hoped SI-6 were holding up their end of the bargain and keeping my mum reassured. I hadn't gone this long without speaking to her since my days on the run.

Ryan had continued to keep a low profile and train with the Zenith team. He'd managed to sneak in a phone call earlier in the day in between sessions.

"Ivan has been pushing us all pretty hard," Ryan had said. "And I could tell a couple of the guys were losing interest, so they've made more of an effort to do fun stuff, like abseiling and that kind of thing. But I've got a feeling that it won't be long now till we're moved inside the mountain." And we both knew what that would mean.

Even though it wasn't the designated time, I took a chance and called BB's number and was really surprised when I got an answer. It was Paddy again.

"I know I'm calling early," I said, "but all the same, I'm really glad you're there!"

"No problem. We were just doing a routine security sweep of our radio systems and I just happened to have your secure channel open. We've realized the encryption on your channel might be contributing to the patchy reception you've been experiencing so I thought I'd better keep an eye on it."

"That would explain the trouble I've had!" I sighed. "Has BB said anything to you? About what I told you?"

"He's made a plan," said Paddy. "Hasn't he contacted you about it yet?"

"No. I was getting concerned."

"He's had a lot on his plate lately. We're pretty sure that SI-6 has been infiltrated—that there's a mole in our organization. BB's been very preoccupied with trying to track them down as quickly as possible."

I was shocked to hear this. "How could this happen in such a secure place?"

"You'd be surprised how often this happens in secret services all over the world. You get someone from the other side coming in, like a legitimate recruitment and before you know it, top secrets are being leaked."

He paused. "But none of this really concerns you, Cal. I wouldn't have mentioned it at all except to explain why BB hasn't gotten back to you. But there is a plan and it's this . . . D'Merrick will come to the island by boat at ten thirty p.m. in four days' time. We're still playing this mission under the official radar so we need to get the timing right to get everything lined up on the quiet. She'll be carrying medical supplies and an extra inflatable so that your people can be safely evacuated. We've seen the reports from Shadow Island about volcanic activity. We want all of you off that island. The state authorities will have warned the Paradise People Resort too, by now. So tell me, what have you discovered about what's going on there? Any more information I should pass on?"

"I hope to have more soon. I still haven't gotten to the bottom of it," I said. "Ryan is working his way through the levels and is almost at the top. I'm hoping that he'll have more in the next couple of days. Tell BB not to send D'Merrick any sooner than that so we can get everyone together to leave. Plus it's our last chance to figure out Damien's master plan. If we can hold on a few more days, perhaps we can uncover more before he realizes we're on to him and vanishes."

I didn't mention the ambush photograph that blew my cover. Not until I knew more about who had taken it. There was nothing Paddy could do about it, anyway.

"OK, I'll let him know. In the meantime, our encryption experts are working hard on that Mordred file," Paddy said. "They haven't told us much so far except to say that it appears to be a series of very complex instructions—algorithms— that are going to need an awful lot of unpacking. Cal, I have to go now. Good luck."

Katz Cave

9:52 pm

I hurried back to the cave and when I went in I found the others still puzzling over the diagrams we'd drawn earlier in the floor.

I was trying to help find some connection between the five plans when I felt my phone vibrate. I looked at the screen and as soon as I started reading the text, I knew it was trouble.

.ntl 3G   9:55 PM

BLOCKED NUMBER

Hey, riddle boy, test your skill on this!
One, two, three, four,
I know what you're looking for!
Part one just for fun . . .
Sometimes it's a place where the ships come in,
Or it cracks a cypher—makes your whole head spin!
Could be found in music—if you like to sing?
Or maybe straight above you—keep the archway in!
Part two just for you . . .
A Long reach after dark that will help you Chase your mark.
In between the resting place, part one stares you in the face.
Tick tock, tock tick 2300 does the trick!
2705
ENJOY!

>MENU   >LOGOUT

I read it through one more time and the second time it sounded even crazier. What on earth was this? The others had noticed the look on my face and they gathered around.

"What is it?" asked Ariel.

"Cal! What's wrong?" Both Zak and Sophie spoke together.

"This," I said and I started reading it out loud.

When I'd read the whole thing to them, I looked up. I saw on their faces the same expression that was on mine—total confusion and bewilderment.

"I have no idea," I said. "The only thing I can think of is that it's from someone who knows that we cracked the Ormond Riddle."

"Who could that be?" Sophie asked.

"It could be almost anyone in the world." I knew that our adventures over the year of chasing down the Ormond Singularity had gone viral. Millions of people had heard about the Ormond Riddle. Once again, I read the text aloud. Once again it did my head in.

"What does that mean?" asked Zak. "It sounds like some kind of nonsense rhyme."

"Whoever sent it reckons it's a riddle," I said. "And a riddle is something that can be figured out." I could tell I was trying to give myself a pep talk.

"Any clue as to who sent it?" Zak asked.

"Nope," I said. "It just appeared on my phone, and it's a blocked number, of course." Someone was sending me texts, but unlike the threatening ones sent by Sligo and his gang when they used to harass me, these didn't seem so menacing. It was almost as if someone was playing with me—tormenting me for sure, but not with lethal intentions.

"One bit seems easy enough," said Sophie, interrupting my thoughts. "'Tick tock, tock tick 2300 does the trick!' is a reference to eleven o'clock at night, surely. Twenty-three hundred hours, right?"

"What about 2705?" I asked. "Is that a postcode? What could it mean?"

"The year 2705 is too far away to be right," said Zak.

"Hang on," I said. "It mightn't be the year 2705. But it could be a date, the month and a day. It could be the 27th of May, for instance."

"So," said Ariel, spreading her hands in a helpless gesture, "at eleven o'clock on the night of the 27th of May, something is going to happen somewhere. Where does that leave *us*?"

"Pretty much in the dark," I said. "But seeing as the text has been sent to me on Shadow Island, maybe we can assume that whatever is going to happen, is going to happen here?"

"That date is in three days' time, so we've got till then to figure it out," Zak said.

No one spoke. "I'm going to forward this text to Winter. She's smart with this sort of thing.

She might see something we haven't."

I forwarded the incomprehensible riddle on to Winter. She called back almost immediately and I filled her in about how the riddle had just suddenly arrived out of the blue.

"Very strange," she said. "It's like someone is hiding behind this, sending you information, but making you work really hard to find out what they mean."

"And I have the sense that someone is playing with me." I told her about being photographed with Ryan near the backpacks under the tree. "Nothing has happened about it since," I said. "Ryan called me earlier. He's training hard. He's really proving to Hamish that he's serious about reaching the highest Zenith level. If that photograph had been shown to Damien, there's no way Ryan would be moving up through the ranks."

"So at least we know your secret's safe for now," Winter said.

"How are you doing with the Mordred key?" I asked.

"Boges says he's made some kind of breakthrough, but he's not talking about it until he's discussed it with Miss Brilliance, the IT whizz at SI-6," Winter replied. "And I spoke to Repro yesterday too, he sends his, and I quote, 'heartiest regards to Cal, wherever he might be, ahem'—there's no fooling him!"

"Good old Repro," I said.

"He was very excited when I mentioned there might be a Scottish connection to your current exploits. His mother was a Finlay, he says, so now he's reading up on Scottish castles. He does love his tunnels and dungeons," she laughed.

"Shame he's not here, I could use a tunnel expert around now," I said.

The moment the call to Winter had ended, Ryan phoned me. Even before I heard the words, I could tell from his tone that he was scared. "Cal! We're getting our implants tomorrow. The others are really excited and I pretended to be, too. No way do I want that stuff put into my arm. But I can't get out of it, either. What am I going to do?"

I felt my brain do a double somersault, before finally righting itself. Remember, I told myself, just one thing at a time. "OK," I said, desperately trying to think of a solution to Ryan's predicament. "I'll come up with something. But you have to get out of it," I said, hanging up. I stared into space for a moment, desperate for inspiration.

"What's wrong? Has something happened to Ryan?" asked Sophie, her blue eyes narrowed with concern.

"He's due to get the implant tomorrow," I said.

Sophie looked stricken. "No! He mustn't! We don't know what's in that Biosurge capsule. I don't trust anything Damien says."

"But then he'll end up locked up, like you were," I said. "I knew this was coming. Why did I let Ryan carry on with this stupid plan? I should have known better!"

"Cal," said Ariel. "Cal! Don't blame yourself. I've got an idea. Ryan was injured before, jumping off that roof—maybe he could get injured again. That way, they'll have to postpone him being part of the final Zenith team."

I nodded, my brain working at the speed of light. An injury—perfect. I called back. "Ryan! Use the Gympie Gympie trees! They put people out of action for months."

"Tell me you're joking! No way am I having the implant, but I'm not going to spend months writhing around in agony either. Get real! There has to be another way."

"I'm thinking, I'm thinking. What if you faked it somehow? Find out what Gympie Gympie stings look like."

"I don't have to research that. I know exactly what they're like! When I was in the sick bay with my injured foot, I didn't have much to look at except the posters warning us about the jellyfish and the Gympie Gympie trees. Mrs. Clayton, the matron, told me more than I needed to know about them. I need to create a raised, red rash and squeal. A *lot*."

"Can you do that?"

"I'll find a way. I have to, Cal!"

DAY 57

34 days to go . . .

Paradise People Resort

10:45 am

Once again, I was heading down the mountainside towards the resort. It was mid-morning and as I approached, I could hear the sounds of Paradise People playing on the various courts inside the fence of the compound.

Through the leaves I could see a game of basketball in session and farther away, I could hear the thunk of racquets from the tennis courts.

Along the beach, there were relay teams doing wind sprints with batons, their teammates jumping up and down in anticipation, ready to grab the batons and run.

Out on the water, on a lazy surf, board riders idled, waiting for a wave, while farther out, some surfboard paddlers and windsurfers tested their skill against the gentle currents and the warm breeze. The scene looked just like the images from the Paradise People's website.

For a few moments I stood and watched because truly it looked like paradise. It was hard to believe that anything terrible could be happening here. From the kitchen buildings, delicious smells made my mouth water as the kitchen staff prepared the midday meal. I suddenly missed my mum's cooking.

As I stood there shaking off thoughts of home, some of the words of the incomprehensible riddle started running around my head in the same way that a phrase of music turns into an earworm that you can't get rid of.

"Sometimes it's a place where the ships come in," kept looping through my mind. "What you're looking for" was "Part one" of that crazy poem. What *was* I looking for? A number of things. A safe way off the island, a way to rescue the stranger locked up on Delta 11 and the prisoners underground, and information about the Mordred file.

There were heaps of things I was looking for. But I couldn't shake that sentence from my mind and found I was even creeping along to the rhythm of "sometimes it's a place where the ships come in."

A place where the ships come in is a wharf, I thought, as I headed towards the end of the compound and saw the long jetty stretching out into the ocean where the ferry docked when it brought in supplies and new visitors to the Paradise People Resort.

A wharf, a jetty, a berth . . . the answer felt frustratingly just out of reach. I just *had* to figure it out.

I made my way along the fence until I could see the administration building where Damien had his office upstairs. I decided that hiding in plain sight was the best way to go, and so moving confidently, I started striding towards the small gates at the rear of the compound. No one challenged me as I walked in. I was hoping that anyone who saw me would presume I was Ryan. I had to get into Damien's office. I needed to look carefully over that board of keys once more, and hope that the key that opened the bunker on Delta 11 was still there and that I could figure out which one would open the iron door that held the prisoners.

I jumped at the sound of someone yelling out. "Hey, Ryan! Weren't you supposed to be at the meeting in the boat shed on the quay ten minutes ago? You better get a move on or Dean will be after you!"

I waved at the fair-haired boy in the striped T-shirt and shorts. The boat shed on the *quay!*

"On my way!" I yelled back. As I said these words out loud, I was singing them in my heart because I *was* on my way! On my way to solving the first part of the riddle that had appeared so mysteriously on my phone. "Sometimes it's a place where the ships come in"—a quay is a place where ships and boats come in. A quay. A quay, or a key. One, two, three, four, someone knew what I was looking for.

I stood rooted to the spot, as the rest of the clues came into my mind—"or it's in a cipher." A *key* is what unlocks a cipher. I started moving, doubling back the way I'd come as the rest of the first part of the riddle unlocked itself in my mind.

What I was looking for could be found in music, according to the riddle; music has *keys* and the last line, something that keeps an archway together, is a *key*stone! Whoever had sent me this riddle, certainly knew what I was looking for! Keys! The key to the bunker cell on Delta 11 and the key to unlock and free the prisoners trapped underground! Someone must have taken them from Damien's office.

As I scrambled away, I pulled out my phone and checked it again.

Approaching the cemetery, I focused on the last part:

> A Long reach after dark that will help you
> Chase your mark.
> In between the resting place, part one
> stares you in the face.
> Tick tock, tock tick 2300 does the trick!
> 2705
> ENJOY!

I couldn't make any sense of the first line, but the second line about "the resting place" seemed oddly appropriate as I looked around the cemetery with its overgrown headstones and weeds growing up between cracked tombs. I was standing in a resting place—*the cemetery!*

Desperately, I started looking around while muttering "a long reach after dark that will help you chase your mark." What could that possibly mean? "In between the resting place, part one stares you in the face!" I'd already figured out that the answer to part one was the word "key." But how could the key be staring me in the face? The number 2300 was possibly an appointed time on the 24-hour clock. But time for what? And what could "a long reach" mean? Stretching out? To what? Or who?

Not even knowing what I was hoping to find, I went up and down, making my way between the graves, but nothing stared me in the face, certainly not any keys. Only vines and lush, tropical weeds which wove their way around and over the crooked headstones. "Sacred to the memory of William Kidney," I read aloud from one of them, noting the odd surname. Fredrick Major, Ernest Shipley, old-fashioned names from a distant past, Ferdinand Longreach . . . I stopped with a jolt. Longreach! "A Long reach" the riddle said. Frantic, I searched all over and around the grave and found nothing but soil and weeds. I had to go back to the others and get their help.

Shadow Island Jungle

11:14 am

I was on my way back up the mountain, my brain working overtime trying to make sense of the last part of the riddle, when my phone vibrated in my pocket. "Ryan? What's happening?" I asked when I heard my brother's voice.

"I'm in the sick bay," he said, "and Mrs. Clayton lent me her phone to call my family." Ryan lowered his voice to a whisper. "Can't talk for long. When I first arrived, a kid showed me this itchy grass that leaves big red hives on your skin. I rubbed that on my arms and it's driving me crazy, but it looks good. And it's gotten me out of having the implant." Then his voice rose to a more normal level. "Mrs. Clayton has asked Damien to take me back to the mainland as soon as possible. I've had some good pain relief, so don't worry, Mum."

Ryan was obviously pretending he was calling home rather than his undercover brother who was hiding in the jungle above the resort!

"Don't let Damien get hold of you," I said. "I'll pick you up as soon as we've gotten everyone together. Good work, Ryan. I knew I could rely on you."

Katz Cave

12:03 pm

Back with the others, I told them about my breakthrough with the first part of the riddle. "Someone is helping us in a really strange way," I said, explaining to them how I'd figured out how the four different clues all delivered the same word—"key." And that the phrase "the resting place" indicated the cemetery as the place where the key might be found. But where in the cemetery?

We went over and over the last section, but we were going around in circles.

"I should tell you," I said, pointing to the words "Long reach," "that there's a headstone in the cemetery for someone called Ferdinand Longreach."

Sophie got it immediately, jabbing at the words.

"Look! Long reach! That's why it's got a capital letter," she cried. "To show that it's a name. And the word 'Chase' also has one. That must be another name. Cal, did you see another tombstone with that name on it?"

"No," I said, shaking my head. "But I didn't check out all of them. I thought I had the answer with Longreach and I spent a lot of time searching all around that grave."

"Who *is* this person who's helping us?" Ariel asked.

"I wish they'd just tell us what we need to know," said Zak. "Why drive us nuts like this?"

"There's no point going back until eleven o'clock the day after tomorrow. That's the date and time we've been given," said Sophie. "I think we should all go. Make a search party."

"What if it's a trap?" asked Zak.

"I've thought of that," I said. "Whoever this person is, they seem to know what we're doing and what we're up to. They could have come and gotten us any time. But whoever it was didn't try to catch us. I'm prepared to take my chances. We need those keys!"

DAY 59

32 days to go . . .

Shadow Island Cemetery

10:56 pm

We had waited impatiently for the allotted time to come. The days had dragged while we fiddled with our supplies, looked at the diagrams and bandied around ideas on how best to rescue everyone and get off the island safely. But we kept drawing a blank when it came to figuring out what Damien was plotting.

Meanwhile, the earthquakes were coming more frequently and I'd never seen the clouds above the island glow like this before. It was becoming more urgent that we release the prisoners under the mountain. If the volcano blew, it might set off the ammunition as well. It didn't bear thinking about.

Finally it was time to go. Keeping our lights as hidden as we could, we made our way down to the desolate cemetery. I couldn't help shivering even though the tropical night was warm. "Up here," I hissed. "This is where Ferdinand Longreach is buried."

Sophie, Zak, Ariel and I clustered around the grave, which was set almost at the edge of the cemetery. All I could see was the mess I'd made two days before, vines and weeds ripped aside. "Let's fan out," I said, "and see if we can find anyone called Chase nearby."

We searched and searched. The time ticked long past 2300 hours and I despaired. I'd wasted all this time when I should have been getting into Damien's office and searching there for the keys that I needed, not stumbling around in the middle of the night in some old graveyard.

"Anyone found someone called Chase yet?" I called out in a low voice. Nobody had.

"We've looked at every headstone," said Sophie. "There's no one called Chase."

Dejected, I went to take one more look at Ferdinand Longreach's tomb just in case I'd missed something. I knew it was useless and even worse, I tripped and stumbled, badly grazing my shin against a stone. I groaned and shone the light onto the cause of my injury. It was a curved stone in the ground on the other side of Ferdinand Longreach's grave. It was an old headstone that had sunk into the earth, probably due to a century or more of earthquakes. I could just make out a name: Marcus somebody. I rubbed soil away from the name and there it was—Marcus *Chase*. Excitement thrilled through my veins.

"Hey, look!" The others surrounded me while I got to my feet, shining more light onto the cleaned-up sunken headstone. "'A Long reach after dark that will help you Chase your mark!'" Ariel quoted.

"'In between the resting place, part one stares you in the face!'" I finished the second line for her. "In between," I muttered, as I started pulling vines and weeds away from between the two graves. I didn't have to dig very deep. A small, plastic-wrapped package lay on the ground. "There's the answer to part one of the riddle," I said, grabbing the small package. "Not exactly staring me in the face, but here it is!"

Hastily, I unwrapped it. Two keys lay in the package—one an old iron key, the other a more modern style.

"This one looks like it came out of the Ark," said Ariel, picking up the iron key.

"No prizes for guessing that it opens the underground door that we think the prisoners are behind," I said. "And this one looks like the modern lock on the bunker cell that holds the unknown prisoner." My strength was returning after the deep disappointment I'd felt just a moment ago.

"Tomorrow," I said, "we're going to rescue some prisoners!"

DAY 60

31 days to go . . .

Shadow Island Resort

8:15 am

While the others were still asleep, exhausted from our late-night adventure, I crept out of our hiding place and climbed a little higher through the jungle. Down at the resort compound, I could hear Hamish's voice ringing out over the loudspeakers, the sound carrying through the rainforest. "Make sure you have all your belongings. We need everyone ready to leave by two o'clock before the bad weather comes in later this evening. The evacuation must be done in an orderly fashion. Please join the others at the beach site to await the arrival of the ferry which will take you to the mainland."

I got the picture very fast. The evacuation of Shadow Island was about to start! The Paradise People were packing up and leaving.

As if to provide more emphasis, the ground shook beneath my feet. I grabbed at some bushy undergrowth to save myself from falling, very nearly grabbing a handful of Gympie Gympie leaves. The pain in my right palm from the stinging modbot had eased considerably. I didn't want to injure myself again. I would need all my strength in the rescue mission to get the stranger off the rocky outcrop and the prisoners out of their underground dungeon. Was Damien going to just leave them there? I wondered where he was and why he was leaving the evacuation to his second-in-command.

"Please remain calm, everyone," came Hamish's voice again, as a small quake shuddered through the ground. "The evacuation is just a temporary safety measure while the volcano is a little unstable. We have plenty of time to get everyone off, no one will be left behind."

"They're planning to evacuate Shadow Island today," I said to the others on my return. "Hamish is organizing it. We've got to move fast. Zak, come with me now. We'll take the smaller key and go out to the outcrop. Sophie, Ariel— take the other key and go to where you think the prisoners are being held. We'll meet back at the cave. We'll have to use the raft and the motorboat to get everyone away." I thought of the submersible, sleek and fast. If only we could get away on that!

I was very concerned that I'd missed my chance to speak to SI-6 and BB the night before. Sophie, as if reading my thoughts, sidled up beside me and whispered, "Cal, I'm worried."

I reminded her of what Paddy had said, that D'Merrick would be arriving to help us with an extra inflatable boat. "Apparently, your dad has been very preoccupied with trying to track down a mole in SI-6. Someone who's been leaking secret information."

Sophie frowned. "Even something like that wouldn't make him forget me—forget about us, Cal. Something's definitely wrong."

9:03 am

After a hurried breakfast, Zak and I headed back down the coast, leaving the girls to make their way to the iron door deep underground. Zipping the key securely in my jacket, I came through the last of the undergrowth to the beach with Zak close behind me. We crawled as quickly as we could along the rocky shore to the mooring cavern. Inside the cavern, I crouched low, heading for the motorboat. We needed to borrow the oars again. I grabbed them from the rocking boat and hurried back to Zak, who was keeping watch at the cave entrance.

Back on the beach, we were relieved to find the raft just where we'd left it, firmly wedged between two sharp volcanic rocks. We had to kick and push it until at last we were able to move it into the water.

The sea, as if troubled by the upheaval in the ground under the volcano, surged and crashed around us. Grabbing an oar each, and narrowly missing being smashed on a jagged ridge of rock, we finally got the raft safely away from the turbulence and onto the calmer waters of the open ocean.

Delta 11

10:46 am

Fifteen minutes of hard rowing and we were pulling the raft up onto the stony shores of Delta 11 once more. We heaved the raft up well away from the water's edge and secured it firmly. I shuddered to think what would happen if we lost the raft. I doubted if Damien would come back to save us. I pushed these dark thoughts away as Zak and I headed for the squat cement bunker a little distance from the shore.

"Hey! We've come to get you! I promised you

we'd be back. We're going to free you!" For a moment I thought there was no one there—or worse, that he'd died waiting for us.

And then a voice, weak at first, but getting stronger, called out. "Is that you, Cal?"

"Yes. And Zak. We're going to get you out of there. We've got the key!"

I ran to the door and pulled out the small key. I pushed it into the keyhole. I turned it. Nothing.

A second try. And a third. Nothing happened.

"Are you there, Cal?" asked the prisoner, anxiously. "What's happening?"

"It's the key," I said. "It seems to be a bit stiff or something."

I was starting to feel a bit panicky. What if the riddler was a joker and this key had nothing to do with this lock?

"Let me have a try," urged Zak, grabbing the key from my hand. Again, he inserted the key into the small dark hole and twisted it. Magically, I heard it click and the key turned. Zak and I grinned at each other. We could scarcely believe it.

We pushed the heavy door and it opened wide. The bearded prisoner, who had been at the barred window, swung around, his wild eyes shining.

The small cement room had a narrow bed, a chair, a desk with an old kerosene lamp sitting on it, and in one corner, a ragged curtain that only partly hid an old toilet and a faucet in the wall.

"I can't believe it!" he cried, coming towards us, arms stretched out. "You came back! You opened the door!"

The three of us stood there in stunned silence for a moment. I could feel a big smile trying to break out on my face, but at the same time, there was a catch in my throat as if I was going to start crying.

The man was tall and lean, and I guess once he would have been a big man and a whole lot heavier. He was too thin, but his eyes now sparkled with life and hope.

"I said I would come back and get you out of here," I told him as he eagerly grasped my outstretched hand with both of his.

"I can't believe it," he said. "I don't know who I am, but right this minute, I don't really care!"

"Come on, sir," said Zak, "we've all got to go right now. We've got a boat coming for us from the mainland . . ."

I couldn't get over how different he was now. The man I'd spoken to through the bars in his cell had been despairing and lost. This man, although hollowed out by his imprisonment and lack of sunshine, was a changed person, alive and full of hope.

"Let's go," I said. "They're starting the evacuation of Shadow Island. Everyone will be leaving today."

The man stopped to gather up a well-used notebook and unhook a very old-fashioned oilskin raincoat from the wall. "That's all I own in the world. I'm ready."

The prisoner walked steadily with us back to the boat, and I noticed his sinewy leg muscles. He helped us pull the raft down to the stony shore and it was obvious that he'd been exercising and built himself up since we'd last come. He even wanted to take over the rowing. Zak gave him his oar and he began to row with me.

"You've no idea," he said, in his still-rusty voice, "how marvelous it feels to be out on the open ocean, with my strength returning, rowing away from that terrible place forever."

I hoped that that his memory might return to him soon, too. We needed to know who he was and why he'd been marooned on that desolate outcrop. As we skimmed across the open sea towards Shadow Island, I asked, "Have you remembered anything yet?"

Without pausing in his rowing, the prisoner shook his head. "It's all a jumble in my mind. I remember a man—but I don't know if it was me or him."

He wasn't making much sense to me. As we approached the rocky shore of Shadow Island I tried another tack. "Does the name Damien Thoroughgood mean anything to you?"

The rowing halted and the prisoner leaned forward, his face alert and troubled. His eyebrows knit together in a puzzled frown.

"Thoroughgood. Did you say Damien?"

I nodded. Zak said, "He runs Shadow Island—the Paradise People Resort."

"Thoroughgood," the man muttered, picking up the oars again. "Damien Thoroughgood," he repeated. "Close, very close. Something very like that is true."

I waited, but he said no more. "Close to what?" I asked. "What do you mean? What's true?"

The man shook his head. "Sometimes I think I'm dreaming. Land sighting—could that be a dream? I have dreams. But this is real, isn't it? It feels real."

"You bet it is," I said, "and so are those rocks!" I steered away from them as strongly as I could, but the waves surged suddenly and it was a battle to edge the width of the raft safely through the craggy sentinels.

Finally, we dragged it out of the surging sea, securing it well out of the water and roping it to the thick trunk of a rainforest tree. I didn't think there was much chance of anyone searching today; it'd be safe there.

"OK," I said to my companions. "Zak, you look after—" I stopped. "We've got to give you a name," I said to the prisoner. "I can't keep referring to you as 'the prisoner.' You're a free man now. As free as you can be on Shadow Island. But soon we'll have you back on the mainland where you can get the right sort of medical treatment that will help you bring your memory back again."

"I'm a free man. Freeman," he said. "That's a good name. Call me Dr. Freeman. Once I was a doctor, I know that much. Not a medical man. But I was a doctor. I can remember my graduation day. I think."

"That's a start," I decided. "I'll go ahead and make sure it's safe. Zak, you follow me with Dr. Freeman—just in case."

Just in case, I thought, his newly recovered strength fails him. After all, he'd just been liberated and goodness knows how long he'd been cooped up on Delta 11. It wouldn't surprise me if it all got too much for him. But so far so good, I thought as I looked back at the two of them making their way along together some distance behind me.

I could still hear the distorted broadcast from

the other side of the island—just the occasional word. It sounded like the evacuation was gearing up, with Hamish giving further orders to the Paradise people. Good, I thought. That means he won't be coming after me and my friends just now. I was desperate to find out how the girls had done with the other key. The fate of the prisoners depended on us. Once we had everyone together—Dr. Freeman, the rescued prisoners, my gang of Ryan, Sophie, Ariel and Zak—we'd be ready to finally get off Shadow Island. D'Merrick's inflatable, together with our raft, and possibly the motorboat if we could steal it, would be our little convoy to safety. The Shadow Island mission would be over.

Shadow Island Jungle

1:04 pm

I was winding my way along a natural track made by a dried-up waterway, which was always quicker than trying to force my way through the jungle undergrowth. The climb around to the big cave was difficult enough without making it harder for Dr. Freeman and I hoped this would be an easier path for him to follow.

I could hear the others behind me when I took a step and then—whoosh! Something grabbed my right ankle and I was flung way up into the air! What the . . ?

There was a bone-shaking jerk and I plummeted towards the ground again!

I yelled in terror as the ground rushed towards me. But astonishingly, my head didn't slam into the earth. Instead, I was jerked back up with a sickening jolt, like coming to the end of a bungee jump. I ended upside down, swinging, caught by one leg, kicking and screaming! I'd been trapped in some snare like a jungle animal. I dangled, thinking of Zak and Dr. Freeman, wondering if they would come to help me, or if they'd stay back, fearful of also being caught.

"OK," said a girl's voice from the nearby undergrowth. "You can stay there until you tell me exactly who you are and what you're doing creeping around in the jungle."

"Let me down!" I yelled. "I'm getting dizzy. Cut me loose."

"No, you'll run away," she said.

"I'm already running away," I said. "Where would I run to now? Who are you? Why are you doing this?" I hoped to keep her talking long enough for Zak and Dr. Freeman to creep up behind this girl who'd trapped me.

"No," she demanded. "You first. You tell me who you are and what you think you're doing."

She had me. If I wanted to get down, I'd have to agree. The blood was pounding in my head as I hung upside down, painfully caught by my ankle while my other leg feebly waved around. There was nothing I could do except cooperate. Up to a point. "OK, OK. My name is Cal. I've been living in the jungle for a few weeks because I wasn't happy here and I wanted to have some time to myself." As the girl glared at me, stony-faced, I knew I needed to be more persuasive. "I'm a bit suspicious about Damien," I added, "and worried about others who could still be on the island. If the volcano blows, they might get hurt. Please cut me down!"

In the silence that followed, I prayed that she would believe me, but there could be no guarantees. So I tensed with terror when I felt a knife at my throat. I struggled to see who this was, twisting my head just enough to see the girl standing behind me, pressing the blade on my neck. "Hey," I said, "go easy with that knife!"

"Listen very carefully. I'm going to cut you down from the snare, which means you're going to fall. It's not very far. But you've gotta stay down on the ground until I figure out what to do with you. Agreed?"

What else could I do but agree? Moments later,

I felt a jerk on the narrow rope that had hoisted me up in the air and then suddenly I was free, dropping to the ground, throwing my arms out to break my fall. As soon as I hit the ground, I rolled over—but I stayed down, crouching, ready to spring away if I had to.

The girl was about Sophie's age, frowning down at me with hard, brown eyes. She looked extremely tough in her khaki shirt, with her black hair pulled back from her pointed face. On her hip was a leather belt and holster, empty now of the knife which she still pointed at me. She gave the impression of being highly trained and athletic. Just under the rolled-up sleeve of her left arm was the Z-shaped tattoo and the small straight scar.

"You're one of the Zenith team," I said, more as a statement than a question.

"Yes," she said, holstering the knife to my great relief. "I'm Georgia Montgomery."

"Spidergirl?"

"How do you know that?" Her brown eyes frowned with curiosity.

"I saw you. Inside the mountain training arena. I saw you scaling the walls. Someone mentioned your nickname."

"I don't understand. How could you see me? I didn't see you."

"It's a long story. I also saw your rucksack with your passport along with the others." I sat up. "I guess it's OK if I get up now?"

She nodded, with a little grunt.

But a noise behind her had her spinning around, the knife in her hand moving in a blur as she leapt back into the undergrowth.

"It's all right, Georgia," I said, "these are my friends. You're safe with them."

Zak and Dr. Freeman cautiously pushed leaves out of the way as they approached.

"What happened?" Zak asked. He turned as Georgia Montgomery suddenly appeared out of the tangle of vines near the dry creek bed.

There was a pause as Georgia sheathed her knife, finally raising her eyes to mine. The hardness had gone out of them. But I couldn't quiet the nagging thought that maybe she'd been deliberately left behind to track us down. Could Damien be *that* devious?

"Why aren't you with the other members of the Zenith team?" I asked, suspicious.

"The short answer is that I couldn't go through with it. I just know that what we're supposed to be doing isn't right. I don't even know really what it is exactly, but every instinct is telling me it's all wrong. At first I couldn't see that."

From deep inside the volcano, another earthquake shook the ground under our feet. The four of us looked at each other. "Georgia, we've got a place that's safe. That's where we were heading when we 'met.' Do you want to come with us?"

"If your safe place is your hidden cave, it's not safe anymore. I saw Dean and one of his cronies going through your stuff this morning," Georgia said.

"Oh no!" Zak was crestfallen. "And we still had those diagrams on the floor," he sighed.

"Don't worry," I said, "we're leaving today anyway. D'Merrick will be here tonight and we won't need the hide-out anymore," I said. "Let's go to the tunnel instead and find the girls."

We made our way slowly through the jungle towards the cemetery. It was a huge risk coming so close to the resort now, but we had no alternative. Luckily, Dr. Freeman was able to keep up with us and Georgia amazed me with her awareness as she constantly watched for danger, her brown eyes alert for anything out of the ordinary. She was like human radar, taking everything in, instantly processing it. I hoped and prayed I could trust her. But I wasn't sure yet.

I was very anxious to get back into the tunnels. Maybe by now Sophie and Ariel had liberated the prisoners and we could find them down here before they went back to the cave. I hoped we weren't too late.

Even with the threat of capture, I couldn't stop thinking that now that we had a top Zenith team member as part of our group, we might find out more about the Mordred key. Georgia Montgomery could be a huge source of information. I hoped she could tell me about the Biosurge implants and the modbots and the reason for the rucksacks—the reason for the eye holograms.

By the time we got back to the secret tunnel, I could see Dr. Freeman was exhausted. Whatever adrenaline he'd been running on had worn off. I made him as comfortable as I could on the floor and left him the lamp. He looked up at me gratefully. "One day," he said, "maybe I'll be able to repay you."

"That's not necessary," I said. "You should never have been locked up out there."

He sighed and smiled at me as he closed his eyes. "You rest now," I said. "We're going to look for our friends. We won't be long."

Underground Tunnels

2:37 pm

I set off with Georgia and Zak, hoping to be able

to find the girls. It took a few false turns and double backs before we found ourselves near the lab again. I could hear the humming from the automated machines in the lab and a few moments later we'd turned into the low clearing where the rover machine stood, still pressed closely against the rock wall where I had abandoned it last time.

"Not far to go now," I said as we approached the lab. As I looked in through the window in the door, the automatic lights switched on inside.

"Hey," I said. "The modbots have gone! And the rucksacks too!" I had a hunch that the holographic eyes would also no longer be in the light cupboard.

But as we made our way past the lab and into the darkness of the tunnel, something Boges had said played on my mind. *Modbots could organize themselves.* Had the modbots been added to the Zenith team rucksacks? What could they possibly need them for?

With the light from my flashlight, I shepherded the others along until we came to another tunnel. We made our way towards where I could hear voices—Sophie and Ariel! Thank goodness!

Sophie hurried towards us, her face concerned. "Cal! What are you doing down here? And how come *she's* here?" she said, looking around me to

Georgia, who glowered in the darkness.

"The cave has been discovered so we need to hide down in the tunnel. We got the prisoner from Delta 11 and Georgia is a runaway now too," I explained. "But what's happening?" I asked. "Did you get everyone out? Did the key work?"

"Cal, I don't know how to tell you this," Sophie's voice quavered in the gloom. Ariel looked wretched. "The key—it broke off in the lock," Sophie continued. "Now there's no way we can open that door. We could hear them thumping on the door this time!"

I could feel my body slump. We'd done so much, gotten so near to rescuing everyone. With a full-scale evacuation going on and a volcano that was getting more and more restless, getting the prisoners out had become even more critical. But the key had broken and I couldn't think of how to get through that door.

"I've gotta get out of here to think," I said. "I need some fresh air."

Shadow Island Jungle

3:10 pm

I scuttled across the cemetery until I found some cover among the jungle undergrowth. I glanced up to see a fiery glow coming from the top of the volcano. I could smell the scent of sulfur and burning vegetation. I *had* to get those people out of their underground prison. Maybe I could find some tools in the stores area that would help break the lock.

I ventured closer to the fence surrounding the resort compound. It looked almost deserted. Elmore was still there, packing up files and boxes. I saw one of the counselors in the distance checking the locked doors and windows of one of the dormitory buildings. I could hear people calling to each other from the beach area so I scampered to a higher position to see what was going on.

I found a rocky ledge that jutted over the beach area, some distance up the mountain. There on the beach, the last few batches of kids, their belongings piled up beside them, waited to be ferried out to a large motor launch that was returning, presumably from off-loading an earlier group onto the mainland. It was still some distance away from the surf. Soon, the evacuation would be complete. I could see Hamish with his whistle gesturing to different kids and I spotted Damien striding around, obviously giving orders.

The earth shuddered under my feet and the biggest earthquake so far caused birds to fly out of the trees screeching and tropical fruit to fall to the ground. I grabbed on to some branches to steady myself, getting tangled up in a Wait-a-while palm and wasting valuable time freeing myself from the tedious hooks. I hated the frustrating plants on the island and couldn't wait to be free of them for good.

Above me, the volcano was rumbling, spewing fiery smoke into the air. Instead of easing, the shaking got worse—it was a *huge* earthquake. I thought of the terrified prisoners locked up in the mountain beneath me. I couldn't wait any longer. There had to be a way to get them out. The iron door was sealing them in to certain death unless I could think of a way. We had no way to cut through the door . . .

For some strange reason the image of the huge circular cutting drum on the front of the robotic mining machine flashed into my mind. If only I could somehow use the blades on that! My mind jumped to the next thought. What an idiot I'd been! Why hadn't I thought of this earlier? We had a huge tunneling machine at our service! The massive mining robot that I'd accidentally activated near the laboratory was exactly what I needed!

Energized, pushing my concerns about Ryan out of my mind for the moment, I scrambled back to Simeon Fincher's tomb, pushed the slab aside and dropped into the hole underneath. This time, I didn't bother trying to manhandle the slab of stone back into position. Thinking of the mining rover had further awoken another memory—the moving pixels I'd seen on the radar screen. Of course, now I understood what they were!

Underground Tunnels

3:28 pm

I hurried back through the dark tunnel to join the others. Dr. Freeman was still dozing and I hoped he was OK and not having some kind of relapse. "Sophie, Ariel? Georgia? I know how we can get the prisoners out! We don't need a key!"

They looked at me as if I was crazy. "I noticed the mining machine's radar screen had moving pixels on it and that didn't make sense because rock can't move. *But people can move!* The radar screen was detecting the movement behind the rock wall. That's where the prisoners are! Come on! Let's find that rock wall again and try some mining!"

Within a few minutes we were back at the wider part of the tunnel which housed the laboratory. This was where I'd seen the pixelated movements. The underground prison had to be a large area because the iron door was some distance away.

Sophie held up the powerful light from the storeroom to reveal the giant mining rover. I needed to drive it purposefully now, not like last time where I'd just banged something and activated the engine.

I stepped up onto the platform in front of the dashboard. It didn't need a driver, but I needed to switch on the engine that powered the massive shearing blade at the front. I turned what looked like the ignition. Nothing happened. I flicked another switch and the massive machine roared into life, startling me. But it wasn't just running its engine. The first switch must have caused the mining robot to rear up so that it could turn. In that moment, a huge earthquake shook everything. I fell against the dashboard before tumbling out of the cab and onto the ground, wrenching my ankle painfully.

Another grinding noise joined the sound of the engine. The robot had completely turned itself around in the narrow space, pivoting as if on a turntable. As I scrambled to get up and out of its way, I saw that the powerful cutting roller at the front was spinning so fast as to be almost invisible, like a powered propeller.

With horror, I saw that it was racing straight at me!

The blazing lights picked me out in the dark tunnel like a rabbit trapped in the headlights of an oncoming car. I scrambled to my feet, scrabbling to run, groaning at the pain in my ankle, desperate to find someplace I could get out of the way of this fast-moving, rumbling monster!

The noise was deafening and its lights were blinding. I tripped and lost valuable seconds getting to my feet again. When I risked a backward glance, I was horrified to see the piercing blades coming closer and closer. If I couldn't get clear, I was going to be minced!

Stuck behind the machine in the narrow tunnel, I could barely hear the girls' screams as they yelled at me to get out of the way. Fuelled by terror, my legs pumped as my eyes cast around the tunnel, desperate to find some little recess or niche that I could squeeze into so that the monster could lumber straight past me. The floor of the tunnel was uneven and stony and I almost fell a couple of times. But there were no alcoves on either side of the tunnel. Blindly, I tripped again and this time it was too late. The dreadful blades were almost upon me. I froze in terror. This was it.

Then, to my disbelief, the massive machine suddenly stopped, just inches away from my shivering body. A miracle had happened. The silence was enormous, broken only by a few stones rattling to the ground. I got to my feet.

Thank goodness, thank goodness, thank goodness, my mind chanted.

Dazed, I shielded my eyes against the blazing light to see Georgia Montgomery standing on the platform of the mining machine, grinning from ear to ear. It was the first time I'd seen a smile on her pointed face. Somehow, Georgia Montgomery had saved me from the monster. Any distrust I might have been feeling about her evaporated.

"Georgia! How did you do that?"

She shrugged. "Emergency shutdown," she said. "I used to help Dad on the harvester." She jumped down, still smiling. "I didn't earn my nickname Spidergirl for nothing," she joked. "I can run up walls, you know. Are you OK?"

"I'm alive, thanks to you. But seriously, how did you do it?"

"I ran fast enough to bounce off the tunnel wall and jump onto the machine platform. Luckily for you, this robot machine has an E-stop just like the one on the harvester."

I got to my feet and together, we climbed back

onto the robotic mining machine. "An E-stop?"

"Emergency stop. See?" she said, indicating two red knobs, one on each side of the machine's dashboard. "Give either one of these knobs a whack and the whole thing simply stops."

I shook her hand. "Georgia Montgomery, I owe you."

"You sure do," she said seriously. "I won't forget it."

"Neither will I."

"OK," she said, "so, how do we make this thing go?"

4:41 pm

It took us a little while to figure out which switches to use for the ignition and to make the machine do its turnaround. But finally, we had it under control and rode on the jolting machine back to the area near the lab where we'd first started.

I explained what I planned to do and they kept back as I studied the dashboard again, trying to find out how to activate the giant mining blades. Last time I'd done it accidentally by falling against the dashboard. I found a black switch labeled *Shear Rotation*. I flicked it on. The huge rotating blades came on with a roar, gaining speed. The radar screen blinked into life and in its eerie light, I again saw dancing pixels, despite the radar being directed at a wall of motionless rock.

Slowly, the machine edged itself closer to the rock wall until finally, with a blistering noise, there was contact as steel bit into rock, and dust and gravel went flying. That's when I realized I should have been wearing protective clothing, but there was no chance of that now. I pulled my hoodie over my head, trying to protect myself from the flying dust and debris churned up by the massive blades.

The machine shuddered as it pressed its cutting blades farther into the rock. Another deafening noise made me look up to see that rocks were falling from the ceiling and that the whole tunnel was vibrating and shuddering. Ariel and Sophie grabbed each other as the earthquake strengthened and Zak looked worried. Dr. Freeman was looking around in a dazed manner as if he didn't know where he was or what was happening.

But I concentrated on what I was doing. I wondered what the people on the other side of the rock face must be thinking. They must be scared, I thought, and they'd have no idea that part of the noise they were hearing was actually the sound of their rescue. The machine kept pressing forward, deeper and deeper. The earthquake stopped and now the only sound was of the shearing blades as they drilled through the solid rock in a perfect circle.

A sudden jolt and I was thrown forward. The machine was through! It had finally penetrated the thick rock wall and cut through to the other side. Through the thick dust that filled the air, the perfectly round hole it had carved out of the rock wall was visible. Beyond, a dim light glowed. I activated the reverse movement and the mining machine backed away from the rock face.

I cut the power and there was an unearthly silence broken only by a small shower of stones. Cautiously, I stepped down off the machine as the others came closer to the opening.

The worst of the choking dust settled, although the area remained hazy with small particles. I could hear people coughing on the other side of the rock wall.

"Hello?" I called through the opening. "Are you OK in there?"

Sophie, Ariel, Zak and Georgia followed me as I crawled through the large hole. I stepped into a long gloomy area. At first I couldn't see anybody and then slowly, what I thought was a dusty pile of rocks in the farthest corner of the room started moving. Gingerly, three figures stood up—a boy and two girls—dressed in grubby clothing, coughing in the dust that filled their long, narrow prison. Beyond them I could see the other side of the iron door, locked forever with its broken key.

"Who are *you*?" asked a thin girl with lank long hair as she tightly gripped the hand of the other girl, a shorter, stocky kid with dusty red hair.

"I'm Cal Ormond," I said, "and these are my friends, Sophie, Ariel, Zak and Georgia," pointing to them as they climbed through after me and stood nearby. "We're going to get you out of this place."

The tall boy wearing a ragged T-shirt and jacket with dark hair pushed back into a ponytail spoke, "I don't know how long we've been locked up, but it's been weeks and weeks—maybe even months. I'm Quan."

". . . and I'm Sabina and this is Artemiz," said the thin girl, indicating her redheaded friend. Then she promptly burst into tears. "I'm just so pleased that someone's come to get us. We've been terrified by the earthquakes."

"We thought we were going to die down here. That we'd never get out," Artemiz whispered.

"We're still not in the clear," I said, "but at least we've got a chance now." I quickly looked around their prison. Just like on Delta 11, there was only a rickety table in one corner and a few stools. Opposite that was another curtained-off area through which I could see a toilet and a sink. A faucet stuck out of the rock lower down with a bucket underneath it. I couldn't imagine what it must have been like, stuck down here, for weeks on end.

"Come on," said Sophie. "Let's find somewhere safe to hide until our friend D'Merrick comes. While we're waiting, maybe you could tell us about everything that happened to you and why Damien locked you up."

The three ex-prisoners didn't have anything much to take—a comb and a couple of jackets. In a moment, they had all climbed through the gaping hole in the rock.

It was clear that none of us wanted to be underground a moment longer than we needed to be, not with the shocking and increasingly strong earthquakes. Even Dr. Freeman seemed to have more energy after his rest.

So with Zak and Ariel leading the way, we all made our way through the cobwebbed tunnel, pausing only for Zak and Ariel to retrieve their bows and arrows. We were quite a tribe now—Zak, Ariel, Sophie, Quan, Sabina and Artemiz, Dr. Freeman, Georgia and me bringing up the rear.

I was struggling with mixed emotions—I was relieved that we had been able to free the three prisoners, but increasingly worried about Ryan. I hated myself for not going to find him before. He hadn't responded to text messages I'd sent earlier and now I had my doubts that there would be much reception with the volcanic disturbance and the approaching storm.

Finally, we emerged through Simeon Fincher's tomb—Artemiz, Quan and Sabina looking around in amazement as they climbed out into the convict cemetery.

Soon D'Merrick would be here and we could leave Shadow Island for good. The volcano rumbled long and deep. Time was running out.

Shadow Island Jungle

10:32 pm

Night had fallen and I was glad of its dark protection. I was worried that our large group would be obvious if anyone was still looking for us, so we waited, hidden, in overhanging jungle growth near the ledge that I'd used to scope out the resort before. From this high vantage point, I could see part of the Paradise People Resort compound. Only a few lights remained, and it seemed quiet and deserted. The last of the resort residents had been evacuated. Now there was only our group anxiously awaiting the arrival of D'Merrick.

I'd still not had any response from Ryan. I hoped he had kept up his act in sick bay. Mrs. Clayton seemed to be a kind woman. With any luck, he'd already been transferred safely off the island with the other resort kids.

I introduced Georgia Montgomery properly to my friends. "She ran away from the Zenith team at the last moment."

"I remember you," Sophie said. "You taught some of the abseiling classes when I was just starting my training with The Edge."

"Why did you run away?" asked Ariel. "Did you object to the implant like we did?" Then she saw the scar on Georgia's arm and the "Z" tattoo. "Oh, you *did* have it," she added.

Georgia nodded. "I was cool about that. And I really wanted the tattoo that went with it. I worked hard at being the best I could be. But later, I started thinking about all the secrecy and I just couldn't get rid of the gut feeling that something was really wrong."

Quan, Sabina and Artemiz all spoke at once. "That's exactly how we felt," said Quan.

"None of us wanted the implant," said Sabina.

"But Damien wouldn't let us go," Quan added.

"We threatened to report him when we got back to the mainland."

"Big mistake," said Artemiz. "He tricked us and locked us up." She looked more closely at Georgia. "You've got the implant and tattoo so maybe it's not that bad after all. How did you get away?"

"We were boarding the submersible this morning," she said, "and we all had strict instructions and sealed orders that we weren't to open until we were in position and the command came, and we were each given this creepy looking hologram of an eye . . ."

The eyes, I thought. They *are* part of the Mordred business! "I was at the back," Georgia was saying, "and as the others boarded, I finally decided I didn't want to be a part of Damien Thoroughgood's great plan to save the world, whatever it might turn out to be."

"Save the world?" I asked, frowning. "How were you going to do that?"

"I'm not sure of the details," Georgia said, "but I know the plan is huge and in some way it will cut pollution by almost three quarters. So Damien says anyway."

That sounded good. Why would he not broadcast such a plan to the world? Why not get people on board with it? *Why all the secrecy?*

Georgia's voice interrupted my train of thought. "We were told that our sealed instructions would include all we needed to know at the right time. I was getting more and more nervous. Then I saw my chance as we were boarding and Damien was up in the forward cabin. I just bolted. I had to leave my rucksack behind, though. I don't know what happened after that because I did the Spidergirl climb of my life and hid in a crevice in the rock ceiling not far from the main tunnel. No one thought to look for me up there in the roof. Damien was furious. When I was sure that they had all gone, I crept out, stole some supplies and hid in the jungle for a while. I was making a camp near the creek bed and I'd set a few traps to make sure nobody sneaked up on me. That's when you, Cal, stepped right into one."

During the rest of the questions and answers, I noticed Sophie and Ariel looking more and more anxious. Dr. Freeman, no doubt exhausted from his sudden freedom and rowing exercise, sat resting, staring into space.

I told them about my conversation with Paddy and how D'Merrick was coming to get us all off the island.

"Who's D'Merrick?" Georgia asked.

"She's a friend," I said carefully.

Sophie and I quizzed the others. "What can

you tell us about the Mordred key?" I asked.

"You've got the name wrong," said Sabina. "We heard Damien talking about something called the *Arthur* key."

"That's right," said Georgia. "I heard him talking about that, too."

The Arthur key? Sophie and I looked at each other. We'd never heard of this one. "What did he say about this Arthur key?" I asked.

Georgia cocked her head to one side, thinking. "I overheard him talking to Hamish one day when we were going into dinner. I just remember him saying 'They'll do anything to get hold of the Arthur key!'"

"You're a hundred percent sure he didn't say Mordred key?" I asked.

"No way. It was definitely Arthur. I don't think I would have confused those two very different words."

I believed her. "What about Melehan?" I asked, recalling the odd name from the Zenith lists of names and numbers.

"What's that?" Georgia said.

I could see she didn't have a clue. "What about you guys?" I asked, turning to Quan, Abbie and Sabina. No one knew.

"We didn't make it to the top level like Georgia did," Quan said.

Georgia frowned. "And what's this Mordred key you're asking about?"

"I wish we knew," I said. "Tell me exactly what Damien told you about what you were supposed to be doing after the training and the implants."

Georgia looked uncomfortable, fingering the straight little scar on her arm beneath the tattoo. "We promised never to say anything."

"Georgia," said Sophie, her blue eyes kind, "a person who makes you promise about something bad doesn't deserve such loyalty."

"But he said we would be doing such a good thing—helping to save the planet from exploitation and pollution. He said we would be like angels on earth, heralding a new age for the world. We would be helping to stop polluters."

"Exactly how was this going to happen?" I asked.

"That was totally secret. Our job was to get to our positions and wait for further instructions. He wouldn't tell us any more than that."

"Where were the 'positions?'" I asked.

"For me, it was London. We were sworn to secrecy about our ultimate destination, so I don't know who was going to what other places. I had a ticket to London, and money and a passport—well, I used to have them—but my rucksack's gone on the submersible without me. I was told there would be another member of the Zenith team who would meet me there. Then we could open our sealed letters which would contain the address of a website we had to log on to for further information about the final stage."

"Do you know anything about the final stage?"

"Not really. Apparently that information will be given to us—to them—once they log on to that website."

"What about the modbots?"

"I know they were packed in everyone's rucksacks. Damien said we'd be told what to do with them once we got our final instructions."

So the modbots *did* play some part in Damien's plan—but how?

I'd hoped for a bit more information than this. I still had no idea where they fitted in. *They can organize themselves.* I leaned back, trying to make sense of what Georgia was saying. A whole new element—the Arthur key—had suddenly come into play. Somehow, King Arthur and his knights *did* have something to do with Shadow Island. Damien was using their names as some kind of code to hide—what? A plan to save the world from pollution? I didn't believe that for a second. And Georgia didn't seem that convinced either.

Another earthquake shuddered under my

feet adding to my feelings of agitation and restlessness.

"Hey!" Zak cried. "Did anyone else see that? A light flashing out at sea?"

I strained forward to see what he was talking about. Sure enough, there was the light again—one, two, three—quick flashes and then darkness. A few minutes later we saw the three flashes again. D'Merrick was signaling that she was heading our way!

I breathed a sigh of relief. As the minutes had ticked past, I'd become worried D'Merrick might not show. Help was finally on its way. But now I knew that I had to be sure Ryan was safe. I should have checked before. But there was still time.

"OK, guys," I said, as I flicked another text message to Ryan, "you go down to the beach and wait for D'Merrick."

"But what about you?" Zak asked.

"Yes," Sophie said, "aren't you coming with us?"

"I'm going to look for Ryan. If he's been evacuated with the others, he's safe for the time being. But I've got to be absolutely certain that he's left the island. Don't worry. I'll join you as soon as I'm sure."

I left them as they started to make their way through the jungle down to the beach while I split off, heading for the Paradise People Resort compound.

Paradise People Resort

11:48 pm

In the night sky, Shadow Island's volcano threatened violence. A huge roar and a great fiery spurt of molten earth geysered up into the night sky, obliterating the stars. I coughed as the air filled with smoke and the smell of sulfur.

My feet flew along the jungle paths I knew so well now. But an unfamiliar sound stopped me in my tracks. I spun around, trying to locate the source of the whistling that grew louder in a split second. Too late, I looked up to see a shower of lava hurtling towards me. I dived under a large tree just as the molten rocks and splatterings of lava hit the ground behind me.

I was up and running again without hesitation—I was out of time.

It didn't take long to get down to the fence that surrounded the compound. I was surprised to see the gates standing wide open, but I guessed that there was no one left to go in or out now. The place seemed completely deserted. Perhaps I was worrying unnecessarily and Ryan had already left safely on the ferry for the mainland. But I had to be sure.

As I looked to the beach, I saw the figures of my friends together with Georgia, Artemiz, Sabina and Quan, and the stooped figure of Dr. Freeman bringing up the rear, making their way across the beach towards the small craft that was nearing, dimly visible in the fiery light of the volcano. Any minute now, D'Merrick would land. As if to reinforce my sense of urgency, the volcano ejected another sheet of fire into the night and the whole island trembled.

I raced to the sick bay and looked in the darkened room. The bed where Ryan had been "sick" was upended on its side, bedding thrown everywhere and a lamp knocked over. What had happened?

Alarmed, my heart started to race as I retraced my steps and ran back to the open gates of the Paradise People's empty resort. "Ryan! Ryan?"

An echoing silence was all I could hear. I called out again, running closer to the administration building containing Damien's office. The doors downstairs were open wide and I ran inside, taking the metal steps two at a time, yelling his name at the top of my voice. Even Damien's office door stood open. I ran inside to a scene of complete destruction. What on *earth*? The computers were smashed to pieces, furniture trashed on the floor. The garbage can was on fire and I could see the charred remains of paper files. Damien had destroyed all the evidence of his plan.

The volcano rumbled again and this time, the building wobbled in a terrifying manner. I grabbed on to shelving which came away in my hands. I rushed to the window that overlooked the beach. I needed to get down there fast or I'd endanger D'Merrick and everyone else as they waited for me.

Shadow Island Main Beach

11:57 pm

I sprinted as fast as I could for the beach. I'd get D'Merrick and the others to take shelter in the jungle and wait while I finished looking for Ryan. As I pushed through the last of the trees and came out at the far end of the beach, a blinding light from the resort tower behind me suddenly threw its harsh beam onto the sea, shining on D'Merrick in her boat. She was already standing up, maneuvering her bulky little craft to the shore. There she stood, completely exposed, as she lifted her arm to shield her eyes from the searchlight's harsh glare. What was happening?

A sound in the bushes to my left made me swing around. Ryan was stumbling towards me onto the beach.

"Thank goodness, bro," I said, about to rush to him. "You're safe!"

He wasn't.

Damien appeared behind Ryan, and I could now see the pistol he held to the back of my brother's head.

"Stop right there! Do exactly what I say, *Cal*," commanded Damien, a triumphant sneer on his face, "and your brother gets to live."

Ryan's eyes filled with fear.

A loud crack pulled my attention away for a split second and as I turned back to look at the others down the beach, I saw D'Merrick, her braid swinging wildly, as she wobbled sideways, tumbled out of the boat and plunged into the sea. She'd been shot!

We had been betrayed. It had all been for nothing.

"If you hurt my brother . . ." I warned.

"You're in no position to threaten *me*," hissed Damien. "If you want to have any hope of getting out of here alive, you'll do exactly as I say."

He nudged my brother viciously with the barrel of the pistol. "The Ormond twins—completely at my mercy."

He pushed Ryan farther onto the beach.

"Now that I have your undivided attention, let me tell you what's going to happen next."

IS RACE AGAINST TIME 06:48 07:12 05:21 RACE AGA
CE AGAINST TIME SEEK THE TRUTH... CONSPIRACY
ONE SOMETHING IS SERIOUSLY MESSED UP HERE (
:07 06:06 06:07 MISSING WHO CAN CAL TRUST? SEE
05 MISSING 06:04 10:08 RACE AGAINST TIME 02:27
EK THE TRUTH 01:00 07:57 SOMETHING IS SERIOUS
RE 05:01 09:53 CONSPIRACY 365 12:00 RACE AGAIN
17 MISSING WHO CAN CAL TRUST? 01:09 LET THE C
GIN MISSING HIDING SOMETHING? 03:32 01:47 05:0
T THE COUNTDOWN BEGIN 09:06 10:33 11:45 RACE A
:48 07:12 05:21 RACE AGAINST TIME RACE AGAINST
E TRUTH... CONSPIRACY 365 TRUST NO ONE 06:0
SERIOUSLY MESSED UP HERE 08:30 12:01 03:07 06
SSING WHO CAN CAL TRUST? SEEK THE TRUTH 12:0
:04 10:08 RACE AGAINST TIME 02:27 08:06 10:32 S
:00 7:57 SOMETHING IS SERIOUSLY MESSED UP HE
NSPIRACY 365 12:00 RACE AGAINST TIME 04:31 10:
N CAL TRUST? 01:09 LET THE COUNTDOWN BEGIN
METHING? 03:32 01:47 05:03 MISSING LET THE CO
EGIN 09:06 10:33 11:45 RACE AGAINST TIME 06:48 0
AINST TIME RACE AGAINST TIME SEEK THE TRUTH
S TRUST NO ONE SOMETHING IS 06:07 SERIOUSLY
RE 08:30 12:01 05:07 06:06 06:07 MISSING WHO C
EK THE TRUTH 12:05 MISSING 06:04 10:08 RACE A
:27 08:06 10:32 SEEK THE TRUTH 01:00 07:57 SON
ERIOUSLY MESSED UP HERE 05:01 09:53 CONSPIRA
CE AGAINST TIME 04:31 10:17 MISSING WHO CAN C
THE COUNTDOWN BEGIN MISSING HIDING SOMET
05:03 MISSING LET THE COUNTDOWN BEGIN 09
GAINST TIME 06:48 07:12 05:21 RACE AGAINST
TIME SEEK THE TRUTH... CONSPIRACY 365
NG IS 06:07 SERIOUSLY MESSED UP HERE (
06:07 MISSING WHO CAN CAL TRUST? S
NG 06:04 10:08 RACE AGAINST TIME 02:2
TRUTH 01:00 07:57 SOMETHING IS SERIOU